THE GAME MASTER
Summer Schooled

THE GAME MASTER

SUMMER SCHOOLED

BY MATT & REBECCA ZAMOLO

ILLUSTRATIONS BY CHRIS DANGER

HARPER
An Imprint of HarperCollins*Publishers*

To the Zamfam, who were the inspiration for this book.
Each of you is special and unique in your own way.
Thank you for being on this journey with me.
—RZ

THE GAME MASTER
Summer Schooled

CHAPTER 1

The Voice on the Loudspeaker

Becca

Don't end up in summer school at Hidden Vista Middle School. Why? Because it stinks. Becca Zamolo had learned that the hard way. One broken leg and an entire quarter of sixth grade missed got her a one-way ticket to humid classrooms and sticky seats and having to do homework instead of gymnastics camp.

Such terrible . . . awful . . . horrendous bad luck.

Instead of doing somersaults, Becca spent four mornings a week *back* in school, melting from heat and boredom. And today was the ultimate worst. They had to redo math class because Matt Darey, Becca's pesky next-door neighbor, got them all in trouble yesterday. He thought he was so funny programming his robot to make jokes during independent work time and they were all being punished for laughing. The whole class was told to come back on the one off-day they had. Unlike regular school, summer school wasn't supposed to meet on Fridays, but this week, because they'd been busted for not listening, Mrs. Gupta insisted that it would. "You waste my time, I waste yours," Mrs. Gupta had said.

But even still, on this particular Friday, the classroom was weirdly almost empty. Only six of them were sitting and waiting for school to begin. *Were the other kids skipping?* Becca wished she was the type of kid who could do that. She was just too nervous to break the rules. Besides, she had to present for their big school project, and she was excited to show off her nana's heirloom zoetrope. An animation reel from when animation wasn't even invented. That was the only bright spot.

Everyone had to bring an object that showcased something mathematical and she bet that no one had anything like it. Becca set it down carefully on her desk, inspecting every part, making sure she'd loaded the animation reel into the barrel correctly. Just like she'd seen her nana do when she first showed Becca how it worked. "It was the first stop motion animation," her nana had explained. "When you look through the slits, you'll see the images moving from the motion. Like a tiny cartoon."

Her nana had let her borrow it under the strictest of rules.

1. **No fiddling with the parts.**
2. **No touching the reel strip.**
3. **No liquids or food of any sort near it.**
4. **No fooling around with it.**
5. **Bring it straight back home right after school.**

Becca was determined to make sure she got her nana's prized possession back safely.

She started to practice her speech: "The zoetrope was invented by mathematicians in the eighteen hundreds and it—"

"Where's Mrs. Gupta?" Matt asked as he stood up and gazed around the room. He clutched that stupid robot, Ralphie, that had gotten them in trouble to begin with. He'd been talking nonstop about it all summer. It even had big round blue eyes and spiky golden "hair," just like his. This morning, Matt had already been annoying everyone by teaching it to sing songs like "Happy Birthday." On repeat.

"Why would you bring that again?" Becca said, pinching the bridge of her nose in anger.

"It's for *my* project," he replied as the robot waved in her direction.

"You're going to get us in trouble. Again." Becca rolled her eyes.

"The bell's about to ring," Matt announced.

"The bell . . . the bell . . . the bell," the robot repeated.

No one answered. Becca surveyed the room. Hiding behind a camera, Danny Watson was too busy videoing Miguel Córdova's pet snake, Nacho, trying to get it to hiss on cue. Miguel hammed it up as the snake slithered its way up and around his arm, settling in on his shoulder. Miguel had spent all of summer school so far complaining that he was missing baseball camp. But everyone here was missing something.

"I taught it Spanish," he said. "You have to say *siseo*."

"How does a snake teach you about math, anyway?" Becca asked.

Miguel flashed her with a gap-toothed grin. "I brought these cool walkie-talkies that my mom got for me and my sister. People used to use these. They're two-way radios. So, like, radio waves." He clipped both to his pants. "But Nacho is extra credit. Symmetry and shapes. Come see her skin— unless you're afraid."

"I'm not afraid of anything." Becca bluffed a little.

"Snakes carry disease," came Kylie Dao's voice. Her long jet-black hair framed her face like a curtain. She leaned forward on her desk, busy drawing a map from one of her travels. She was the only kid Becca liked in summer school. Kylie usually flew off to visit family in Vietnam as soon as school let out. But summer school had ruined those plans, too.

Miguel brought Nacho around from desk to desk, basking

in everyone's squirms and squeals.

"It'd better not eat my cheese. I need it for my project." Frankie DiMarco, rocking their ever-present skinny jeans despite the heat, had arranged five different snack containers on the desk: Gouda, Parmesan, mozzarella, cheddar, and was that blue cheese? Whatever it was, it stank.

Becca stared at the clock on the wall, watching the seconds tick by slower than a turtle. It was nearly eight now, and Mrs. Gupta was never late. Any minute now, she'd come rushing in, bells jingling on the beautiful silver sandals she always wore. Same basic outfit all summer. Those silver sandals and a long flowy skirt. She also rocked a pair of perfectly round glasses that accented her perfectly round face. Becca thought she looked like a tawny owl. She was a good teacher, though. Summer school was a tough assignment for anyone, and Mrs. Gupta did her best to make it not horrible. But where was she?

The bell rang, a warning, and Becca pulled out her notebook, ready to write down any announcements before math started.

Matt peered out of the classroom and into the hallway, then turned back around. His pale cheeks reddened. "Where *is* everyone?"

Becca looked up. Matt was right. Their classroom was still super empty. Kids should've flooded in by now. Every seat was usually taken. But it was just the six of them.

Matt got up.

"You're going to get a demerit for being out of your seat," Becca warned.

He ignored her, peeking his head out of the classroom. "No one is in the hall," Matt reported, frowning. "No one's *anywhere.*"

"So what?" Frankie replied while admiring their tower of snacks, scrawling proportions and ingredients into their recipe notebook. "Gives me more time to perfect this Leaning Tower of Cheese-a. Get it? Mrs. Gupta's gonna love it. A-plus for me. She can whip out her protractor. So many angles. See? SEE? Also, maybe it'll count as a recipe for when I enter the *Kids' Cook-off across America.* Could be in my back pocket for one of their challenges." Frankie chuckled to themself, then nibbled on the block of cheddar from their stack. "I could make a tower as high as the ceiling or something."

The late bell rang, echoing through the empty halls, signaling the start of class. Mrs. Gupta would keep them as punishment since no other students were here.

Becca was worried now. Mrs. Gupta should have been up at the front of the room, going through announcements for next week. Usually, there weren't that many. Noon dismissal reminder. Homework folders. Parent info fliers. The daily letter from Principal Collins.

And today there shouldn't really be any since they weren't supposed to be here.

Matt paced the room, then took his seat.

They all sat at their desks.

Becca stared at the clock.

8:00 a.m.

8:01 a.m.

8:02 a.m.

Mrs. Gupta was never late. She would make you stay after dismissal for every minute of hers that you wasted.

8:03 a.m.

"If no one comes after five minutes, we can leave," Matt proclaimed. He'd barely been in his seat a minute, and already he was itching to move again.

"How do you know that?" Becca challenged.

"It's a rule." Matt walked to the front of the classroom.

"Says who?" Kylie said, finally looking up from her map.

"My older brother," Matt said, nosing around Mrs. Gupta's desk.

Becca stood and walked toward him. He was always causing trouble. "What are you doing?"

Miguel let his snake coil around his arm while Danny ducked and weaved between the classroom desks, capturing every moment on video. "What should we do if no one comes? How does that make you feel?" Danny asked. "Tell the camera."

Matt looked under Mrs. Gupta's desk and then in her closet.

"She probably isn't hiding in there," Becca said.

"Her briefcase isn't here. Also, her running shoes. She always puts on those ugly sneakers after school." Matt scratched his head, ruffling his dirty-blond hair.

Danny went into the hallway, filming the empty halls like he was collecting evidence. "No one is in the other classrooms. I'll use my camera's motion sensor to see if it picks up on anything."

They all followed him and looked around. Becca darted to the other sixth-grade summer school homeroom, overseen by Mr. Jenkins.

Empty. Of course. It's an off-day. But where would Mrs. Gupta be? Didn't other teachers come in to grade and stuff when kids were out of school?

Danny ran down the hall toward the seventh-grade classrooms. He turned around and shook his head. "Nobody!"

Kylie peered out one of the big windows. "I don't even see anyone out there." She turned around and started shouting, "Mrs. Gupta? Mr. Verdi? Principal Collins?"

Nothing.

No answer.

Weird.

"We can leave!" Matt shouted with a fist pump in the air. "I'll get more time to work on my robot. Time to teach him more commands. I'm outta here."

They all raced back into Mrs. Gupta's room.

But Frankie froze. "Who ate my project?"

Everyone looked at Frankie's desk. The Leaning Tower of Cheese-a was reduced to one sad and lonely cracker. Each one of the snack containers sat empty.

"Who did it?" Frankie's light brown cheeks reddened. "Someone ruined it." They looked accusingly from one kid to the next. "What am I supposed to turn in now?"

"We were all in the hall," Becca said. "There's no way any of us could've eaten your snacks."

"One of you must have sneaked back in here . . . while we were looking around," Frankie said.

"I didn't do it," Kylie said.

"Neither did I," Matt replied.

"I'm allergic to cheese," Danny added.

"What about your snake?" Frankie asked Miguel. But the snake was still perched on Miguel's shoulder.

"Maybe it was the robot, Ralphie?" Frankie glared.

Ralphie burst into another rendition of "Happy Birthday" at the sound of his name and Matt leaped forward to shut him down. "He doesn't like cheese," Matt said, shoving the robot into his backpack.

Frankie stamped their foot. "Who was it, then? Someone was in here. Someone took it."

"Nobody wanted your cheese," Becca replied.

"It's now been ten minutes," Matt said. "I'm outta here." He grabbed his bag, and the rest of the kids started to pack their stuff up, too.

Becca went back to her desk to get the zoetrope and her backpack. She'd tell her parents what happened. Maybe she could make the eleven o'clock tumbling class she had thought she would miss. But then she noticed that her nana's heirloom wasn't where she'd left it. She ducked and looked under the chair, then behind the desk beside hers. Her heart hammered and her stomach twisted. *Where was it?*

"Guys, this is not funny," she said as the other kids started toward the door. "Give it back."

"Give what back?" Danny asked, the camera clicking as he started to shut it down.

"My nana's zoetrope was here on my desk, ready for my presentation, before we went out in the hall. And now it's not here—" Becca swallowed hard. "It's not funny. Give it back now."

"What's a zoetrope?" Kylie asked.

But before Becca could explain, the loudspeaker crackled. Finally.

Everyone glanced up at the speaker in the corner of the room, waiting to hear about the school day and what was happening.

And then a deep scratchy voice announced: "Who wants to play a game?"

CHAPTER 2

Your Mission Awaits

Matt

Matt stared up at the loudspeaker, unsure that what they'd all just heard was real. Did someone really ask if they wanted to play a game? His heart raced. What was happening?

His eyes darted around the room. Kylie nibbled her bottom lip, more confused than creeped out. Frankie's mouth hung open. Becca turned bright tomato-red. Danny clutched his video camera to his chest. Miguel whispered to his snake, asking if it was okay.

Matt started to pace again, his robot clutched tight to his chest. "I told you we should have bailed, like, twelve minutes ago."

Frankie, still annoyed about their missing cheese, walked

to the wall and shouted up at the loudspeaker. "Who are you?"

"Nacho is getting nervous," Miguel said as the snake hissed toward the loudspeaker.

"We really should get out of here." Kylie stuffed her maps into her backpack and stood, ready, as always, to bolt.

"What about my nana's zoetrope?" Becca asked, resuming her search around the room again. She checked the bookshelves and their cubbies, all empty. She checked under Mrs. Gupta's desk, all empty. She checked in the supply closet.

Matt had seen her nana's zoetrope every time his mom dragged him with her to visit Becca's mom. Becca wouldn't shut up about it. Even though he usually hated *everything* Becca liked, he had to admit it was kind of cool, but he'd never let her know that.

"I can't find it. I can't find it," Becca repeated over and over again.

"And my snacks," Frankie added.

Matt checked his backpack again to make sure his robot hadn't gone missing, too. He patted the top of Ralphie's head. Phew! He was safe!

"No one cares about your cheese," Danny added, grabbing his camera. "I should document this for evidence." He zoomed the camera across the room, poking into this corner and that. "I don't see the zoe . . . zoe . . . that thing." He shrugged. "What is it again?"

"We've gotta get out of here," Matt said, louder this time. "That voice was weird."

"Yeah," Kylie added. "It was too deep. It definitely wasn't Principal Collins." Backpack loaded, Kylie darted for the classroom door, but it slammed in her face. "What the . . ." She tried to turn the doorknob. "It's locked!"

"Huh?" Matt raced over and tried the doorknob, too. "She's right."

"Did you think I made it up?" Kylie snipped.

"No, it's just—" He tried punching numbers on the door's keypad. Nothing.

The loudspeaker crackled again.

Everyone froze and looked up.

Laughter leaked from the loudspeaker.

"Is this a joke?" Miguel yelled out. His pet snake was hiding her head in his tank top.

"Who *are* you?" Becca shouted. "This really isn't funny."

The classroom SMART Board clicked on. Its blue glow washed over Mrs. Gupta's desk. A logo flashed on the screen: big and white with the letters *GM* and the words *Game Master* taunting below them.

"It's time to play a game," the loudspeaker said. "Especially if you want your precious possessions back."

A picture of the zoetrope appeared on the screen. It was definitely the one that belonged to Becca's nana—black and round, like a giant tin can, painted with a pretty blue paisley pattern on the outside, with little slots inside to hold the film cards. They watched it spin on the screen as an echo of laughter got louder, louder, louder. It was super creepy.

Sweat beaded down Becca's cheeks. Matt started to feel bad for her.

Someone had definitely taken the zoetrope. But who? And why? He knew if she didn't get the zoetrope home in one piece, she'd be in major trouble. Probably grounded for life because her dad was like his dad—no nonsense.

"Give me my zoetrope back!" Becca yelled at the loudspeaker. "It doesn't belong to you."

"Who are you?" Miguel yelled.

Frankie walked up to the screen, poked at it, and watched as it rippled.

Danny grimaced. "Don't! You'll break it."

Kylie tried the door again, her face hopeful. But it was still locked tight.

Matt looked behind the screen, hoping to find the culprit. "Nothing." He shrugged.

"I'm the Game Master." The voice on the loudspeaker laughed again.

The Game Master, Matt thought. *What the heck is that?*

"Pay close attention!" the voice demanded.

The SMART Board flashed and a big bold message appeared.

THE SCHOOL IS YOUR ESCAPE ROOM.
FIND THE CLUES.
FIGURE OUT EACH PUZZLE.
EARN NANA'S ZOETROPE BACK—
AND YOUR WAY OUT.

"What's an escape room?" Danny asked.

"My moms took me and my family to one last month for my sister's birthday. You get locked in a room and you have to work together to get out," Miguel explained, clutching his snake close.

"Ugh, please no," Frankie said, frowning. "I did one last summer, and it was awful. We were locked up for hours until my cousin finally figured out how to get free."

"I'm not playing any games. I'm getting out of here," Kylie replied. She tried to yank the door open.

The loudspeaker voice laughed again.

"Just give me back my nana's zoetrope!" Becca shouted, her fists balled at her sides.

"C'mon, whoever you are!" Matt yelled back. "It's important. Give it back."

This wasn't his idea of a good joke. Usually, Matt was into games, making people laugh, or at least freaking them out a little. It was one of his favorite things to do. His family called him the Mattster, prankster extraordinaire. But his were way better than this, and he never stole things. Like at

15

the beginning of the summer when he'd put spiders in his parents' shower and recorded his dad screaming like his baby brother or last week when he'd hidden all the doorknobs and made his mom think there was a ghost in the house.

But he'd never trap anyone in school. That was *not* a way to get a laugh. Not the good kind from deep down in your belly.

"Let's see if you can trust one another long enough to find it," the voice said. "Maybe you'll get the zoetrope back . . . and maybe you'll just get to leave. Only time will tell."

The sound of a clock ticking echoed through the room.

"But starting now . . . the clock is ticking. Tick tock, tick tock."

Becca was shaking.

The whole class stared in horror at the SMART Board as the eerie white Game Master symbol flashed again on the screen.

CHAPTER 3

There's No I in Team

Becca

Becca's cheeks felt red hot. She had to get the zoetrope back. All she wanted to do was give her presentation, finish summer school, and get back to her *regular* life: gymnastics, the pool, hanging out with Nana, and trying to convince her dad to help her build a clubhouse in the backyard. This wasn't what she had signed up for.

The worst part of it would be breaking her nana's trust. She couldn't bear the thought. Maybe Nana would never forgive her.

But she couldn't find her zoetrope alone.

"Is this one of your pranks, Matt?" Becca challenged as she

paced around the classroom, her hands pressed to her forehead as if she were trying to hold back a headache. "Promise me."

He scoffed like she'd just accused him of stealing a million dollars. But he was always up to something.

She peered into hidden corners, still looking for her nana's heirloom. It had to be here somewhere. Matt played tricks on her all the time. Once he snuck into her yard to dump ice cubes in her pool. He'd leave dog poop where she'd be sure to step in it and send "anonymous" letters from aliens, which were so obviously written by him. She hated that their moms were best friends.

"It's *not* me, I promise," Matt answered. But Becca didn't believe him. Not one bit.

"Anyone recognize the voice?" Frankie asked.

"It's not Principal Collins," Danny replied.

"Of course it isn't her. Why would she do this?" Kylie replied. "We don't even know it's a real person." Kylie poked at the SMART Board, but it didn't turn back on.

"It's not a ghost. Like, that's a real person's voice," Frankie said.

"But whose?" Becca asked.

"What are we going to do?" Miguel asked, his voice rising. "How do we *escape*?"

"We've got to look for clues, I think." Danny started to walk around the classroom, camera perched on his shoulder.

"Maybe my camera can pick up unusual activity. We can review the footage. It helps sometimes to show things we might not otherwise notice."

Frankie riffled through their backpack. "I'm calling my sister. She'll come let us out. This is too weird."

"Maybe we should call the cops, then?" Miguel said. "It's missing, so you can file a report or something. Maybe they can find it."

"This is a crime scene," Danny added, nodding. "Let's gather the evidence." He zoomed in close on the desk where the zoetrope had been. "They'll have to sweep for finger-prints."

Frankie fumbled with their phone. "Uh-oh."

"What?" Becca asked.

"My phone doesn't work." Frankie held it up, tapping wildly. "Someone else try theirs."

"I don't have a phone. My dad won't allow it," Matt said.

"Mine either," Kylie chimed in.

Miguel, Danny, and Becca took theirs out. They tried to make calls.

"I have no signal," Danny reported.

"The school internet is down, too." Becca tried to hold the phone high above her head to get something . . . anything. But nothing.

"There's no way out of this." Miguel's voice sounded afraid.

Becca rushed over to them. "What if I don't get my nana's heirloom back? What if it's gone forever?" She could feel tears pooling, threatening to spill. But she couldn't let herself cry. Matt would never let her live it down. "I'll be grounded forever."

"Maybe the zoetrope is just hidden in here," Matt said. "What does it look like again?"

Becca clicked through the pictures she'd taken of it this morning, showing everyone. Seeing it made her want to cry again. Worries fluttered in her stomach. But Becca knew there was no time for tears. She had to focus. "We have to work together to get out of this."

She turned to the group, trying to figure out the best plan. "Danny, you scan every corner of this space with your camera." He ran off to start. "Then we'll review it after a few minutes to make sure we didn't miss anything."

"Kylie, map out where the zoetrope was, and the rest of the room," she ordered as Kylie sat down, pulling out a fresh sheet of paper. "Frankie, go get the Tupperware and let Miguel and the snake sniff for prints." Did snakes sniff? Maybe that was just dogs. Whatever, they needed to figure this out. She was desperate. The door was their only escape. The windows were designed to open just a crack, barely wide enough for even Nacho to fit through. "Matt, try the door. And keep trying different codes." If they all worked together, they'd be able to figure this out. They had to.

She'd never worked with them as a team before. Not a group project in class. Not even during gym. She hoped they could do it.

Everyone darted around the room, working, following her orders, in their own special way. But as the minutes ticked by, they didn't find the zoetrope—or the cheese. And they couldn't unlock the door, even though Matt and Miguel kicked at it, pulled at it, pushed at it. They tried everything.

Becca paced and searched, one eye on the clock as it *tick-tick-tick*ed.

She glared at Matt and Miguel, who were already getting distracted by the snake and making faces for Danny's camera.

She stared at the door, willing it to open. Then she noticed the keypad. There was something on it. Something almost translucent. When the right light hit it, there was a hint of a picture. That's when she saw it. The GM symbol.

"Wait!" Becca knelt in front of the door and ran her finger over the keypad, feeling the slick and smooth surface of a sticker. "The keypad."

"There's always a keypad," Kylie replied. "All the classroom doors have one. So what?"

"Yes, but it has the symbol on it. That strange GM." Becca pointed. "Maybe it means something."

Everyone rushed forward to have a look. Miguel tried the doorknob again. It didn't budge. Kylie tried kicking down the door. Frankie punched a bunch of random codes. Danny examined it from every angle.

"Okay, let's try different combinations. Maybe our birthdays," Becca directed. "Frankie, write them on the board."

"Why would anyone know our birthdays?" Miguel asked.

"Do you have a *better* idea?" Becca replied, her foot tapping, the anger rising inside her. Each moment they were stuck in here and her nana's zoetrope was missing felt like forever.

Frankie grabbed a piece of Mrs. Gupta's chalk as everyone shared their birthdays. Matt started punching the codes in. The door didn't budge.

"Now what?" Matt asked.

"Maybe we try the numbers on our school ID cards?" Kylie offered. "Or the school address? The classroom number?"

Becca started to pace again. This was a game. She'd always been good at games.

She ruled at Monopoly and always beat her cousins at checkers. Her mom had even started teaching her to play chess this summer. Mom said Becca was destined to be the family champ. And she loved their annual scavenger hunt when they went camping. This felt different, though. She could figure it out if she calmed down. She thought about the advice her mom always gave her: "Take it slow, map it in your head, do the math. Look for the patterns." She pulled out her notebook and started writing.

A stomping noise pulled Becca out of her thoughts. She glanced around at the rest of her classmates, wondering who was doing that. Kylie was writing down combinations on the chalkboard as the boys shouted random numbers that didn't immediately make any sense to her. Frankie combed through the room, looking for numbers that might pop up here or there, offering a clue. Danny filmed them all as they did it, directing them to move this way or that.

The noise was starting to give Becca a headache.

"I can't think with the stomping. Who's doing that?" she snapped.

"Not me," Miguel said.

"Or me," Matt added, watching his robot scoot away.

"Or me." Danny turned his camera around and faced her.

"I'm trying to cross off all the codes we've used," Kylie added while on her tiptoes writing more and more of them on the board.

Frankie frowned. "I've been looking for codes and clues." They shrugged. "We're all just trying to help."

Becca frowned and turned back to her notebook, continuing to scribble down all the possibilities.

The stomping started again.

Everyone froze.

"You hear that?" Becca whispered.

"Yeah." Kylie and Miguel said in unison as they started to search for the source.

"It's probably just the pipes," Matt said, staring at the chalkboard full of codes. "We need to just keep trying different combinations."

"The pipes only make that kind of noise during winter. With the heat." Becca put her ear to the wall. "Wait. I think . . . I think . . . it's a pattern."

Danny videotaped her. "I'll be sure to get this footage in case it stops."

"That's two stomps, then a pause, then seven more," Becca said to Kylie.

"Five more," Miguel chimed in.

"Now back to two," Frankie added.

"Eight," Kylie replied.

Then the room went silent.

"What does this have to do with anything?" Matt asked.

"What if it's part of the puzzle?" Becca challenged with her hands on her hips. "What if it's a clue to escaping *this* room?"

"Or what if it's just bad pipes?" Matt rolled his eyes.

"Then you won't have a problem with us trying it?" Becca marched right up to him and plucked the chalk out of his hand. "What was the code again?"

"Two. Seven. Five. Two. Eight," Danny reported, while replaying his footage of the stomps.

Becca scrawled each number on the board:

2 7 5 2 8

"Try this?" she asked, holding her breath as Frankie pushed the numbers. She squeezed her eyes shut and waited to hear the tiny hum of the lock turning.

But nothing.

"Ugh!" Matt punched the wall. "Told you it was the pipes."

"Wait, wait. Shhh!" Danny set his camera down and pressed his ear against the wall again. "Kylie, you listen closer to the door."

She scrambled and also pressed her ear to the wall.

"Some of the taps are longer than the others," he reported. "Can you hear that?"

"That's why it's not a clue." Matt grabbed his robot and almost threw himself into his chair.

Danny repeated the beat on the wall. "Just wait."

"Is it a song?" Miguel asked.

"I don't think so." Danny tapped again.

Becca's heart pounded. Where had she heard this noise before? It was so annoying. Becca tapped it on the nearest desk, then repeated the noise. "Mrs. Gupta."

"What about her?" Frankie asked.

"She always makes that sound." Becca started to pace.

"Gupta code, remember?" Matt called out.

Mrs. Gupta would always make certain sounds at the beginning of class before the morning warm-up, and kids could crack the code and leave their theories in her extra-credit box. Then they'd get math bucks to use for points on a quiz or test.

Becca ran to the box glued to the wall and rifled through it. Inside, she pulled out a piece of paper that said, MORSE CODE. "Look!"

Everyone rushed over. Becca's eyes scanned all the lines and dots.

"What's Morse code?" Miguel asked.

"It's like how they used to send messages and stuff back in the day." Danny made one of the noises with his mouth. "That's SOS. Like if your ship got lost. If you're in Gupta's class during the year, she always uses it. A combination of dots and long stretches."

The noises started again.

"Shh," Becca whispered, waving Kylie to the board. "A dot for one beat and a line for the long sound."

$$\cdot \ \cdot \ \cdot \ - \ -$$
$$- \ - \ - \ - \ -$$
$$\cdot \ \cdot \ \cdot \ \cdot \ \cdot$$
$$- \ - \ - \ \cdot \ \cdot$$
$$\cdot - \ - \ - \ -$$

The classroom went silent.

"Okay, that's it, I think," Kylie said.

"Now, we've got to decode." Becca gazed up at the board while Danny called out the patterns. Her heart pounded as they lined up each dot and circle according to the code on Mrs. Gupta's sheet. "Three, zero, five, eight, and one."

"Frankie, try the door." Danny pointed.

Frankie punched the code in.

The door buzzed and clicked open.

They were free!

CHAPTER 4

Copy That!

Matt

"Let's get out of here!" Matt barreled through the door with his backpack and robot. Everyone followed him. He shoved right into the entrance's double doors and bounced back. His robot went flying through the air, and he covered his eyes in horror, expecting the worst. But thankfully, Miguel caught it before it hit the floor. Matt quickly packed Ralphie safely away.

But then Kylie and Danny barreled around the corner and crashed into him with a thud.

"Ah! My camera!" Danny shouted, cradling it close. Kylie rubbed her shoulder, mumbling under her breath angrily. Frankie, ever amused, paused to laugh before running down the hall to try the door near the stairwell.

Also locked.

The kids all ran through the hall, trying every classroom door, shouting and screaming as they went.

"Help! Help!" Matt screeched at the top of his lungs. But not a single door opened. And not a soul answered them.

Nothing.

They were stuck in the hallway now.

Danny tried his phone again. Still no signal.

The loudspeaker crackled to life again. Everyone froze. "You're still playing my game," the weird voice declared.

"We don't want to play!" Kylie shouted.

"Let us out!" Frankie hollered.

"Aren't you having fun yet?!" the voice answered. "And it's the only way you'll get back your nana's precious zoetrope, Becca!"

Everyone stared at each other, their faces full of fear and irritation.

"What's a zoetrope again?" Matt asked.

Becca sighed, exasperated. "You've seen it a dozen times. I can't believe—"

"Just kidding," he joked.

She scowled at him. Maybe that was bad timing. But when he got stressed, the jokes always poured out. He couldn't help it.

"You know, that tin can thing Becca had," Miguel said.

"The one that's missing?"

"I know, I know," Matt replied.

"Also, don't forget my project, my cheese." Frankie grimaced. "One of you guys owes me twenty dollars' worth." They frowned at Matt, who smiled, trying to not look guilty like his mom always claimed.

"Guys! Focus! The zoetrope! I really need to get it back," Becca pleaded. "What would you do if they took your snake, Miguel?"

He clutched Nacho tight to his chest.

"Or your robot, Matt?"

Matt's eyes bulged. He clutched the robot close. He'd be so upset.

"Or your camera, Danny? All that footage lost."

"They already ate all my cheese!" Frankie interrupted, glaring at Matt.

Becca burst out laughing, and the others joined in.

"What?" Frankie exclaimed.

Becca shook her head.

"So what should we do?" Kylie asked, tapping her foot.

"What choice do we have? Get out of the escape room. We win the game and get our stuff and get out of here!" Becca said. "Are you with me?"

Kylie stepped forward first. "I'm in."

"Me too," Danny replied.

"Me three," Frankie added.

"Yeah, okay." Miguel lifted Nacho to his ear. "We're in!"

Becca turned to Matt and cleared her throat. "Ahemmm!"

Matt inspected his robot.

She cleared her throat again. He finally looked up at her; his nose felt hot and pink, his forehead sweaty. *"Fiiiiiine!"*

"Okay, so we work together and play the game. We get my nana's zoetrope back and then get out of here as quick as we can." Becca waved her hands in the air.

Matt leaned against the door, plotting in his head. There had to be a way. A simple solution. He just had to—

The lights went out with a loud click, all at once, plunging them into darkness. Miguel screamed.

"Look!" Matt pointed, walking forward. "There's a shadow in the hall." He took off running.

The shadow moved quickly.

"Hey! YOU!" he shouted. The rest of the kids followed.

His footsteps pounded even faster than his heart. But as soon as he turned left down the hall, he lost the shadow. "Where'd it go? Did you see it?"

Out of breath, Miguel replied, "I can't find it."

Becca leaned against the wall, panting. Frankie, Danny, and Kylie sprawled out on the ground.

Matt looked left and right, wondering if whoever had set up this game was right behind them, lurking and waiting. Shivers ran down his back, the little hairs on his neck standing like tiny terrified soldiers.

The loudspeaker crackled again, and the familiar voice boomed. "You have your mission, not quite impossible. Figure out how to escape and you might just get to enjoy the rest of your summer—but fail, and you'll be summer schooled forever!" The voice cackled long and hard before the sound faded again, leaving them in an eerie, dark silence.

Who was the Game Master? Who would do this? If there was one thing Matt Darey didn't like . . . it was not knowing things. Matt stared down the long empty hall, wondering what to do next. *What did this person want?*

Frankie started tugging at one door after another. Matt put his robot down to help, pulling the doors in case somehow magically one would open. Frankie glared at him. But it didn't matter. Not one door would budge.

"What are we going to do?" Kylie asked.

"We need to find whoever this is," Matt said.

"But what about my nana's zoetrope?" Becca started to pace.

"If you let me finish . . ." Matt rolled his eyes. "I think we should split up. One team does the puzzles and the other investigates whoever this person is. You still have those walkie-talkies, Miguel?"

"Yeah," he replied, taking them off his hip.

"Kylie and Danny with Becca." Matt pointed. "And Frankie and Miguel with me."

"Why do you get to make the groups?" Becca jammed her hands to her hip.

"Look!" Kylie shouted. "Those stickers again." A series of Game Master stickers glowed on the floor in a path leading down the hallway. "I think we're supposed to follow them."

"We don't have time to fight about this," Danny said, looking pointedly at Becca. "Let's just listen to him this time."

"Fine," Becca said.

"I'm not *that* bad," Matt replied, trying to get everyone to smile.

Becca rolled her eyes. "Whatever."

Miguel handed her one of the walkie-talkies and showed her how to use it. "Let's practice. Go down the hall and turn it on."

"Frankie, Miguel, and I will try to get clues or find this person. You all report back." Matt clicked the side of the walkie-talkie. "Copy that."

Becca scowled but nodded her head.

"You're supposed to *say*, 'Copy that,' back." Matt grinned at her.

The group split up. Becca, Kylie, and Danny started to follow the stickers down toward the gym doors.

Matt led the others down the opposite hall. He tugged at the classroom doors, but they didn't budge. "Dead end," he said, but Frankie slid past him and tried the others.

"There's something in here!" Miguel called out, pressing his face to the glass windows of the teachers' lounge. "A cup of something . . ."

"So what?" Matt replied, trying to think through where to go next.

"It's still hot. I can see the steam." Miguel opened the door. "That means—"

"Someone was just here or is close." Frankie hustled behind him.

Matt dropped his book bag and raced to follow. "Wait for me!"

He held his breath as they tiptoed into the off-limits teachers' lounge, ducking beneath a sign that read: No Students Allowed. Long rows of computers and desks clogged the center of the room, and refrigerators and snack machines lined the left wall.

"Whoa," Frankie said. "Look at all these snacks they get. No fair. We don't even have machines in the cafeteria." They ran their fingers over the glass machines, salivating. "Teachers get everything. Anyone have change?"

"How can you think of your stomach at a time like this?" Miguel asked. "We need to get clues and get out of here."

"It's, like, nine thirty. Time for second breakfast." Frankie smiled.

"A what?" Matt and Miguel said in unison.

"It's not even lunchtime." Matt scowled at them.

"I like a second breakfast. Like those hobbits." Frankie waved their hands in the air. "My sister and I read the book. I made all the food from it." They pressed their cheeks to the glass of the machine. "Even when it's lunchtime, I won't have anything to eat. 'Cause someone ate my lunch." They shot a stare over at Matt.

"Not me," Matt told them. "I don't know what happened to your cheese, but I know I didn't take it. It was stinky."

"Fiiiine!" Frankie turned back to the machine.

"We need to look for clues." Matt went from row to row, scanning the teachers' desks. Many were so messy. Pencils and pens, stacks of paper, old textbooks and workbooks. And they had the nerve to complain about his locker and desk. The nerve.

"Hot chocolate!" Frankie shouted.

"Not this again." Matt didn't even look up.

"No, no. Come look." Frankie dragged Miguel over to a corner desk. "Matt! C'mon."

Matt sighed and walked over. "What is it? Your stomach again?"

"It's still hot." Frankie waved their hand over it, wisps of steam curling between their fingers.

"So what?" Matt's brow furrowed. He didn't understand what hot chocolate had to do with any of this. "Like, who even drinks hot chocolate in the summer? Isn't that, like, against the law? It's too hot."

"It means someone was just in here," Frankie said, skulking around, checking every possible area as if the person might be hiding under one of the desks or in the coat closet.

Miguel lifted the cup. "Even more than that. Hot chocolate is Mr. Thomas's favorite drink. Remember in science last year when he showed us the chemical reaction required to make hot chocolate?"

"So?" Matt replied.

"So I think it's a clue. Maybe he's behind this." Frankie tapped at the papers under the cup. "There are school blueprints."

"But why?" Matt combed through everything, his mind full of suspicion. Mr. Thomas was one of the teachers he actually liked. Also, he wasn't teaching summer school this time around, and Matt would know because somehow he always ended up in summer school because he always forgot to do his homework. He was too busy with his various *projects* and he wished teachers would've just learned that by now.

"Maybe he is upset with us for being in summer school?" Miguel continued to search the desk.

That didn't feel like a big enough excuse to go through all of this trouble.

"There's a list here"—Miguel held it out—"with all of our names on it."

CHAPTER 5

Finding the Right Path

Becca

Becca kept a count of the Game Master floor stickers. Twenty-six so far as they snaked through the hall toward the gym.

Kylie ran ahead. "They stop at the gym doors."

"Hold on! Almost done." Becca thought maybe the numbers meant something like with the first puzzle.

But Kylie pushed the doors open and clapped with glee. Becca wiped her brow. Finally, something had gone right.

They ran inside, the door slamming behind them. The sound of a click echoed. Becca whipped around and pushed against the metal handle. The doors were locked.

They were stuck in the gym.

"Uh, guys, this is weird," Danny declared, staring into the

darkness of the gym, and flipped a light switch on his camera, and they all gasped in shock.

Mountains of school furniture were piled up in all directions: tables and chairs, desks, file cabinets, whiteboards and SMART Boards, tubs of school supplies and books, art easels, science lab tables, and more.

Becca pressed the side of the walkie-talkie. "Hello?"

"You have to say, 'Becca to Matt,'" Kylie corrected.

Becca scowled.

"That's how they do it on TV."

"Ugh, okay." Becca repeated Kylie's line.

"Hello," came Matt's voice on the other end.

"We're stuck in the gym. Door's locked. Can you help us?"

"We'll be there as soon as we can," he replied. All this noise echoed behind him. "We've found something."

"Okay." She released the button.

"You're supposed to say, 'Copy that.'" Kylie smiled.

Becca rolled her eyes. "You deal with it, then." She handed the walkie-talkie to her before turning back to the mess in the gym. "Principal Collins is going to be majorly mad." She let out a low whistle.

"It's how they wax the floors," Kylie chimed in. "They put all the stuff in here as they work their way down from the top floor."

If her nana's zoetrope was in here, Becca would never find it. It was a minefield. "How did you know about the furniture?" Becca challenged.

"My sister volunteered last year at the soccer camp. She saw the custodian, Mr. Verdi, and his team moving everything. The school even paid her a few bucks to help," Kylie reported.

"Oh," Becca said, easing deeper into the maze of stuff.

Danny scoped the scene with his camera, filming the massive pile and zooming in and out, looking for clues.

Kylie pulled a notebook from her bag. "It is getting super hot in here."

"The air conditioner's off," Becca said.

"Yeah," Danny said, not nearly as stressed about it.

"You really think it's in here? That tin-can joey-trope thing?" Danny asked, starting to dig through things. "Come on, guys. Help me look. The quicker we find it, the quicker we escape."

"It's called a zoetrope," Becca corrected. "I'm thinking it has to be here somewhere." Becca turned to everyone. "Here's the plan: Kylie and I will keep looking for the zoetrope while Danny, you look for a key or a clue to get us out of the gym. Cool?"

"Yep, but first, should we check in with Matt on that walkie-talkie thing?" he asked.

"Let's wait until we have something to say first," Becca said. "Okay? Let's split up." She marched to the left with Kylie behind her.

"I'll grab some footage over here," Danny said. "My camera picks up stuff in dark spaces. We'll find it." He winked and nodded at Becca. She watched as he moved straight into the maze of furniture and boxes, getting down on his knees to search. At one point all she could see was the top of his head.

"Hey, this might be something," Kylie shouted, hidden on the other side of the giant pile. Becca leaped up, excited. Then she heard Kylie's voice again, deflated. "Never mind."

It had to be here somewhere. But there was just so much—stuff. Becca started throwing things left and right. Old English textbooks and plastic bags and boxes of broken pencils and tubs full of arts and crafts supplies. Her eyes darted left and right. She would find it. She had to.

There was weird blue tape on the floor, too. Like the kind Becca's dad used when he wanted to paint the walls. She jumped over it in case it would stick to her sneakers. Sweat soaked through her T-shirt, dust coating her legs as Danny scooted past, his camera low to the ground. Far in the distance, Kylie laughed as she ran under the bleachers with a half-deflated basketball, playing instead of helping. Becca tugged again and again at the gym doors, annoyed and hot, too.

"I'm taking a break." Danny plopped down on the ground, sending dust flying in Becca's face. He started reviewing footage as she tried to stop sneezing.

"Bless you," Kylie's voice called from beyond the pile. She slowly made her way around, picking dust out of her dark hair. "Ugh, I'm all sweaty and gross."

Danny inspected the camera lens for dust. "Can we just try to get out of here?"

"We can't give up!" Becca said, sneezing again as she tried not to panic. "The zoetrope has to be here somewhere!" She looked around, frantic. "Besides, we're locked—"

"Wait!" Danny called out. "I think . . . I think my camera picked up on something."

Becca and Kylie raced over.

"There's something silvery." He played the footage for everyone. His brown cheeks were all clammy and sweaty in the gym heat. "See that?" He rewound and played it again.

Becca's heart hammered. Maybe it was the zoetrope. Maybe this whole thing would be over fast. She hovered over Danny and watched the replay. A glittering object peeked out from beneath one of the SMART Boards. "Can you zoom in?"

The camera clicked and the frame widened.

"What is that?" Kylie asked.

"I don't know!" Becca replied.

"It's near that overturned SMART Board." Danny turned and pointed.

Everyone dived back into the mountain of stuff.

Becca ran to the other side. "Next to the desks." She waved Kylie and Danny over. "Come on, guys. Lift."

Becca and Danny lifted the SMART Board and Kylie wiggled right under it, grabbing and scooting.

"I found it," she called out, lifting the object high into the air.

"My zoetrope?" Becca said, squinting.

"Nope," Kylie said, still satisfied. "A key."

CHAPTER 6

Everything's Coming Up Missing!

Matt

"What does this mean?" Matt held the memo with their names on it up to the light.

"Someone set us up. That's what." Miguel pulled more papers from Mr. Thomas's desk. "There's a printout of the email they sent home to the other kids telling them they didn't have to come for Gupta's makeup class." He tapped the paper. "It labels us as the troublemakers. Whoa. Who did this? What a jerk."

Frankie paced back and forth, trying their phone again. "We should go get the others out of the gym and try to leave again. There's got to be another door in this building that leads out."

"I can't think. Hold on." Matt laid all the papers in front of him. The memo with their names on it. The email sent home to the other kids in Mrs. Gupta's class telling them they didn't have to come in. "Who would do this?"

Miguel rattled through a bunch of theories.

"Maybe Mrs. Gupta was tired of us messing up her math class?

"Or making fun of her shoes?

"Maybe Mr. Thomas is working with Mrs. Gupta to teach us a lesson?

"Maybe it's one big April fool in July?

"Teachers can be mean."

"They're not *this* mean," Frankie challenged. "Not Mrs. Gupta. I would've been mad, too. We weren't listening and let *Matt* and his robot get us all into trouble."

"Hey, don't slander Ralphie." He'd just learned that word from his dad while watching court TV shows where people sued each other for the bad things they said.

The printer clicked on.

Matt, Frankie, and Miguel whipped around. Nacho started to hiss. The snake curled around Miguel's shoulder, ducking its small head into his collar. Time felt like it had slowed down as the printer hummed and clicked, preparing to spit out paper. Matt felt his breath catch in his throat. Beads of sweat raced down his back.

He gulped as the paper pushed out into the bin.

"Who wants to look?" Frankie asked.

"You go." Miguel shoved them forward.

"No, *you*." Frankie pushed back.

Matt took one careful step forward with Miguel and Frankie right behind him. His mind raced. *Who could it be? Why is this happening? What are we going to do?*

They stood in front of the printer, looking back and forth at one another, waiting for the other to grab the paper. Matt elbowed Frankie and Frankie poked him back. Miguel tried to move back but Matt caught him. "We do it together, okay?"

"Okay," Frankie squeaked out.

Miguel nodded, and held his snake close to his chest.

They stood before the printer

Matt started a countdown.

"One.

"Two.

"Three."

All three of their hands reached out and grabbed the warm paper.

Matt scanned it.

WHAT MAKES FOR A GOOD FRIEND? DOES TEAMWORK REALLY MAKE THE DREAM WORK, LIKE THE TEACHERS ALWAYS SAY?

IT'S TIME FOR YOU TO TEST IT OUT.
—THE GAME MASTER

"What does this even mean?" Frankie asked.

"'Teamwork makes the dream work.' Who talks like that?" Miguel replied.

"Wait, I've heard that phrase before." Matt took the paper and held it up. *Hmm*, he thought, his mind racing through a thousand possibilities. "Do either of you have Ms. Bhuyian for science?"

"Only once, when she filled in for Mr. Thomas in lab."

"She says this *all* the time." Matt pursed his mouth. "What if . . . what if—"

"She did it," Miguel blurted out.

"Or it's another clue. And it's where we should be going." Matt tapped the paper.

"The science labs!" Frankie exclaimed.

Miguel squeezed the walkie-talkie. "Miguel to Becca."

They all waited for a voice on the other end.

Nothing.

"Miguel to Danny."

Nothing.

Miguel shook the thing, then clobbered it against a nearby desk.

"Careful," Matt cautioned. "Let me try."

Miguel handed it to him. Matt took a deep breath.

"Kylie here," came a voice from the walkie-talkie.

Matt almost fumbled with it before catching it. "We found something. A clue, possibly."

"We did, too. Copy that."

"Science lab," Matt replied. "Did you all make it out of the gym or should we come get you first?"

"We're still stuck, but we found a key," she reported.

"Meet you in the science lab upstairs?"

"Yep. We'll let you know if we need help," Kylie said.

"Copy that," Matt replied.

They darted out into the hall. Matt snatched his back-pack. It felt weirdly light and banged on his back as they started to race to the staircase.

"Wait, wait." Matt stopped and knelt to the floor. He unzipped his backpack, checking to make sure Ralphie the robot was still tucked inside his hoodie, safe and sound. But the book bag was strangely empty. He tore through it, yank-ing out his pencil pouch, notebooks, the sticky Rice Krispies Treat he'd forgotten to eat in June, spare parts for Ralphie, and his tablet. "Where is Ralphie?"

Matt looked up at Frankie and Miguel. They were frozen in place. Miguel's big brown eyes stretched wide. Frankie's light brown cheeks rushed pink.

"I don't have it." Miguel put his hands up.

"Unlike you eating my cheese," Frankie said.

"It's not funny, okay? I didn't. I promise." Matt couldn't

stop the panic from entering his voice. He jumped to his feet and retraced his steps.

His heart thumped so hard, he thought it might jump out of his chest. He also felt like he might vomit. Ralphie meant everything to him. He'd been working on him for the past two years and he hoped one day to create the first robot kid. He was well on his way. His dad even promised to build him his very own lab. But now, Ralphie was missing.

Frankie and Miguel started to help him look. They turned left and right down different hallways.

Matt called out. Ralphie had an autoresponse to him. He should reply, "Right here, Mattster," if he was close by.

The sounds of shoes echoed.

The three of them froze.

"What was that?" Frankie whispered.

"I don't know." Matt gulped.

The sounds got closer and closer.

They gazed down the hall. A large shadow stretched out.

"Who's there?" Miguel yelled out.

No answer.

The shadow got closer. Any second and the person would turn the corner.

Frankie turned and ran. Miguel followed right after him. They screamed for Matt. He took off, too.

The noises of footsteps close behind them.

CHAPTER 7

Keys to Nowhere

Becca

Becca's stomach was in knots as she gazed down at the tiny key in Kylie's palm. It looked so small. Too small to open a door. Too small to be important. What if her zoetrope was gone forever? What would she tell Nana?

Kylie handed it to Becca. They all huddled around, peering at it in Becca's palm.

"Wait," Becca said, rubbing her fingers against the shiny metal ridges. That familiar symbol. The GM logo sticker right there in the key.

"It's part of the game," Danny said. "Has to be." Danny pointed his camera at the sticker, zooming in and out. Becca could hear the click as he snapped his shot.

"But what does it open?" Becca asked.

"You think it's for the doors?" Danny asked.

"It's got to be," Kylie responded.

"Or for these file cabinets," Danny replied.

Becca held the key up. "Could be both!"

"But a key only fits one lock," Kylie challenged her.

"Not if it's a master key. A master key is made to open more than one thing," she explained as they raced toward the gym doors. "My dad got one from the locksmith because Mom was always losing her house keys." Becca tried to insert the key into the door lock. It didn't fit. Too little. Just like she'd suspected. *Ughhhhh!* "But—" She started to argue but swallowed it. She had to keep up the faith.

"Let's try the side door. The one that leads out to the playground," Kylie suggested, reaching for the key. "So we can get the heck out of here."

Becca handed the key to her and they all took off running in that direction, crashing into each other as they skidded to a stop in front of the door.

"Ouch!" Danny grimaced as Becca nearly toppled him. "That hurt."

But there was no time for arguing. Kylie was already trying the key in the lock. She shrugged as she turned back to the others. "Nope," she said. "Not that one either."

"We should tell Matt, Miguel, and Frankie. They can try

to open the door from the outside," Kylie said, lifting the walkie-talkie up.

"Okay," Becca replied, hating to admit defeat.

Kylie pressed the side and said Matt's name three times. No answer. Then she said Miguel's and Frankie's names. Silence. "What's going on?"

"I don't know." Becca's stomach twisted; the nerves piling up.

"Let's try to use the key and wait for them to get back to us," Kylie suggested.

"If it doesn't open the front gym door and it doesn't open the back gym door, what is it for?" Danny riddled as his camera clicked through different modes. "It's gotta open something."

"The file cabinets," Becca said. "Maybe there's another clue in there."

They raced back through the piles of furniture.

"Everyone pull out the file cabinets. Let's line them up and try the key, one by one."

Grunting and sweating and shoving things left and right, they dragged all the black cabinets out of the furniture heap.

Becca tried the key in one cabinet, then the next, then the next. They all opened. But all of them were empty. Was this not the right plan?

"Try the next row," Danny urged, videoing the insides of them.

"There's nothing here." Becca moved at lightning speed, trying to get them all open.

Nothing but a few balls of paper here and there. Trash.

She tried a tenth.

Nothing. Empty.

She tried the twentieth. Another ball of paper. Ugh! Becca slammed her hands on the top of one.

Danny plopped himself down on the dusty gym floor. "Man, I'm tired. What time is it?"

"Guys! Guys!" Becca said, stamping her foot. She couldn't help it. "Come on. Focus. The key—"

"Forget the stupid key." Danny started toward the piles again. "It's probably just garbage. Whoever's behind this probably just left it lying around to mess with our heads." Maybe he was right? But Becca didn't think so. She felt sure the key *had* to be something. It had the Game Master symbol on it. "We should find another door. I mean, the key—"

"What if it's a key to nothing?" Kylie said.

The loudspeaker crackled again, and they all froze. Becca shivered despite the heat. Was the voice going to give them another clue?

They waited.

And waited.

But then there was silence. No voice from earlier.

"What do you want?" Kylie shouted up at it.

"Who are you?" Danny yelled.

They waited again.

"Let's keep looking." Kylie stepped backward and slipped.

"You okay?" Becca asked, barely catching her.

"Yeah." She wiped the sweat off her face.

"Wait!" Danny replied. "There's something here."

Becca whipped around.

He held up a map of the gym and a compass rose. "This is something. There's a Game Master symbol on the side."

He spread it on top of the cabinet. "Hmmm."

But it wasn't a map like Becca was used to seeing. The picture of the gym and all its mess was separated into four spaces with two intersecting lines. In the corner was a legend of tiny symbols and a sketch of the compass rose. "Anyone know how to use that?" Becca flipped the compass rose over. She'd seen them before but didn't know how to use it.

"Yeah, but we don't need it. Feels like something that will slow us down. Or is supposed to throw us off." Kylie tapped the map legend. "It's a quadrant map and you use coordinates to find things."

"How do you know all of this?" Danny asked.

"My dad. He's a cartographer so he makes all sorts of maps. They're like my favorite thing."

"Cool." Danny ran his fingers over the symbols. "But how do we read it? What does it all mean?"

"We need coordinates. There's an *x* line and a *y* line." She pursed her lips and flipped it over, scanning for something Becca couldn't figure out. "This is quadrant one—and two, three, four."

"What do you mean?" Becca asked.

"If we aren't told any coordinates, we can't figure out whatever it's trying to tell us." Kylie scanned the page.

Becca started to pace.

"This isn't working." Danny shrugged again. "Maybe we can climb out the windows?"

They all turned to look at the windows—which were a good eight feet off the ground. How would they even start?

"They're probably locked, actually," Kylie said with a sigh. "If they open at all."

Danny kicked one of the file cabinets. It tumbled over, the paper ball landing at Becca's feet. She picked up the ball, getting ready to chuck it into the mess, but she saw a thick black line. She uncrumpled it and spotted:

(3, 2)
(0, 5)
(6, 4)

"This is it!" Kylie said.

"What do we do?" Becca gawked at the page.

"We split up and go to these points." Kylie led Becca and

Danny out of the edge of the maze of cabinets and furniture. "Look! I should've noticed this before. The blue tape."

"What about it?" Becca's brain raced. Why couldn't she see what Kylie saw? She just felt so confused.

"It's a grid. The tape. There's a method to the madness of the piles, I guess. See?" She dropped to her knees and pointed to a placard taped to the floor. "This is where the office furniture is supposed to be . . . in quadrant one. Books and classroom supplies in quadrant two."

"Oh," Danny replied, zooming in and out with his camera.

"So someone . . . this Game Master person made it into a quadrant grid. Let's go to the coordinates." Kylie stretched her arms out as she counted the different boxes out loud.

"But how?" Becca had just started learning how to plot numbers on grids and in her head it started to make sense, but she felt like being all stressed out made her brain fuzzy.

"I'll show you." Kylie led Danny to the first set of coordinates. "Danny, you look in this section. There should be a clue." Then, she led Becca to the farthest one in the back corner. It was full of classroom shelves and teaching equipment like SMART Boards and DVRs and TVs. "Everyone search. We've been in the wrong sections the entire time."

Becca didn't need to hear any more. She got to work, searching through all the equipment. What could the clue be? Or could her nana's zoetrope be buried over here?

"I found something!" Danny held up an envelope. A Game

Master sticker shined on the front. He tore it open and read, "Ah, you thought this was the right spot! But keep looking and maybe you'll be rewarded." He grimaced. "Ugh!"

"Come help me." Kylie waved him to her section. They disappeared into the junk and Becca turned back to her search. Her eyes scanned and she mopped sweat from her face. What was she missing?

"We've got something, I think!" Kylie shouted.

Danny and she held up a chalkboard. The Game Master symbol was etched in white chalk across the deep black.

The message that was scrawled said:

FRIENDS NEVER STOP LOOKING . . . BUT MAYBE THEY SHOULD START LISTENING?

"UGH! WHAT DOES THAT MEAN?" Becca screamed. Her own voice startled her and she fell backward into a shelf.

"Are you okay?" Kylie scrambled over with Danny right behind her.

Her ego was more bruised than her backside. She sighed and tried to lift herself, her hand hitting an old-style tape recorder. A button clicked and a voice sounded.

They helped her to her feet.

"OMG, what was that?" Kylie asked.

Becca bent down and picked it up. A garbled voice spoke.

"Turn it up," Kylie asked.

Becca fumbled with it. "I don't know how."

Danny took it and inspected it. "My dad uses one to tape himself while he's writing. Says it helps him remember his ideas."

"Can't he just use his phone?"

"He likes to keep it old-school. That's what he says." Danny clicked a few buttons, and the noise of a tape rewinding sounded. He pushed Play again.

The same weird voice from the loudspeaker said, "To find your way out you must find your way in. I have a door but I'm not a car. I have things hanging inside me but I'm not an art gallery. I am sometimes dark, but there's usually some light. I store things but I'm not a shed. I'm much better looking. If I was in your house, I wouldn't be the bathroom, and I would contain clothes but not be the washing machine. I'm actually a place where so many things hide. Especially those who are afraid."

It clicked off.

The three of them stood in silence gawking at it.

"What does that even mean?" Kylie asked. "I'm terrible at riddles."

Becca gulped. Her mind raced. She was good at riddles. During elementary school, her mom used to write one on a napkin every day and put it in her lunchbox.

"I hate this. I just want to get out of here." Kylie scowled.

"I know, I know. Me too," Becca admitted, but she

couldn't leave behind the zoetrope. Not without trying. She played the message again. The voice made the hairs on her arms stand.

"It's a room. Has to be. But which one?" Becca gawked around. "Not the bathroom. Not the locker room because that's where the bathroom is . . . even though you can hang things in a locker. Hmmm . . . not an office."

"There's only Coach Dillon's office left," Danny said.

A jolt shot up Becca's spine. "No. It's the closet."

"What?" Kylie challenged.

Becca pointed at the only other set of doors in the gym. She felt deep down that was the answer and rushed off. The kids raced to follow.

"Ah," Danny said as they stopped short, avoiding a crash landing this time. "That makes sense."

"Of course! It has to be," Kylie said, nodding and making notes on her little pad. "There are no other options."

"But why would we need to go in the closet?" Danny asked. "That's not going to help us escape."

Becca held her breath. It had to be. It had to. "But maybe it's where they hid my zoetrope." She reached for the doorknob. There was a dramatic click, and as she pulled the handle, the doors flung wide open, releasing an avalanche of about a hundred bright red kickballs and basketballs.

"HELP!" Becca shouted, but all three of them were submerged.

The trio made their way through it all.

Becca stared into the darkness inside the closet. A ncon GM symbol shined, marking a spot on a glow-in-the-dark wall map with the title *YOUR WAY OUT!*

CHAPTER 8

Shadows and Hairnets

Matt

Matt, Miguel, and Frankie didn't stop running until they burst through the cafeteria doors. They darted through the maze of draped tables, ducking left and right, attempting to hide.

"Slow down!" Miguel shouted to Frankie and Matt. "Nacho is getting sick."

Sweat poured down Matt's cheeks. He knew his face must be bright red. "Get down. Let's hide over here." He crashed behind the table in the back corner near the double doors that led down to the basement kitchen. He lifted the drape so they could each crawl beneath it. Huddling all together, they made themselves as small as possible to not be seen. Matt felt like he was a little kid again playing hide-and-seek from his older sister . . . but instead someone evil was chasing them. Whoever this Game Master person was.

The walkie-talkie started to crackle and Matt heard Becca's voice. *Oh, no!* He quickly grabbed it and whispered into it. "Can't talk, okay?"

"What?" Becca replied back.

"Message you back in a minute." Matt clicked the Off button as the sound of the cafeteria doors opening boomed through the room. "Shush." Matt put his hand up. "Freeze."

Frankie panted, their cheeks slick with sweat. Matt could feel Frankie and Miguel trembling beside him. Miguel hugged his snake so close, Matt was almost afraid Nacho would be smothered. The snake licked and hissed lovingly.

Matt held his breath as the pounding of footsteps got closer . . . and closer. His eyes were focused on the drape, and through it, he saw the silhouette of legs.

Frankie gasped.

Matt clamped a hand over Frankie's mouth. The panic quivered through both of their bodies. What if this person heard them and lifted the drape? What if this person wanted to hurt them? What if they *knew* this person?

The silhouette walked around the table before heading in another direction. Matt listened as the footsteps tapered off, getting farther and farther away.

"Should we try to follow them?" he whispered. A surge of

bravado flared inside him. Maybe they should just confront the Game Master and get the whole thing over with. "They might have Ralphie. I have to get him back."

"Uh, no way," Frankie whispered hard.

Miguel's brown eyes grew wide.

"We could end this whole thing." Matt scrambled forward but Frankie pulled him back.

"And die! We could end this whole thing including our lives." Frankie shook Matt. "Are you serious? You can't be serious."

"Yeah," Miguel chimed in. "Becca might not get her grandma's thingie back. Your robot is gone. I'm not about to risk Nacho."

Matt's heart thudded so hard, he felt like it might jump from his chest.

"We need more clues. We need to talk to Kylie, Becca, and Danny first. We need to know what we're up against," Miguel continued.

They were right.

Miguel lifted the drape a little and said something to Nacho in Spanish. "I think the room is empty."

"How can you be sure?" Frankie pressed, their thick eyebrows lifting with suspicion.

"Nacho is sensitive to people and loud noises." Miguel inched forward even more. Frankie went to grab his shirt, but

Matt also peeked out of another area. His blue eyes checked the room. It was empty.

"What if that person is hiding from us, too? What if they jump out?" Frankie said.

"Then we deal with it, but we can't stay behind the drapes forever. And we have to go help the others." Matt climbed from under the table, followed by Miguel and a reluctant Frankie. "Split up and look around."

They scoured the room for any clues that might've been left behind. They lifted every table tarp, peeked behind the catering stations and in the cafeteria bathrooms.

Nothing.

Matt felt like it was foolish to keep looking. "Let's go help Becca and—"

"There's my cheese!" Frankie shouted near the kitchen doors.

Matt and Miguel ran over. A messy trail of cheese squares littered the floor. Frankie was on all fours inspecting it.

"How do you know it's yours?" Matt asked. It looked like regular cheese to him. Not that it wasn't strange that cheese squares were scattered all over in the cafeteria, especially when no one was supposed to be in here.

Frankie held one up. "See the tiny holes? I spent hours poking them with tiny holes so I could build my Leaning Tower of Cheese-a."

"Doesn't cheese already have holes in it?" Miguel challenged while Nacho slithered down his leg and sniffed at a piece.

Frankie scowled. "Not these kinds."

Matt followed the cheese path toward the kitchen doors while Frankie gave Miguel a cheese lesson. He tiptoed ahead to the kitchen. His entire life in this school, he'd been told NO STUDENTS ALLOWED back here. Mr. Otto, head of the cafeteria, didn't play either. You took one curious step into the kitchen and it'd be automatic detention for a month. And Matt knew: he'd sent the first Ralphie model back there to get some footage on how their cafeteria food was made. He actually loved the food and just wanted to know why the hot lunch was always so good. But boom, even Ralphie wasn't sneaky enough, and he got caught.

Matt pushed the door open. The kitchen was a mess. It looked like some sort of recipe gone wrong. There was cheese all over the counter. Baking ingredients were set out on the center table. Every pot in the kitchen was lined up.

"What was going on?" he asked the room as if it could answer back. A piece of stained paper sat among the mess.

Matt reached for it, brushing off the sugar and flour and who knows what else. A printed picture of Frankie stared up at him.

WHO IS FRANKIE DIMARCO?
"Cooking is like a big experiment with food, like science class!"
1. *Food*
2. *Baking*
3. *Cookbooks*
4. *Science*
5. *Cheese*

It reminded Matt of those old-fashioned Wanted posters, but instead of all the bad things Frankie had done, it was all the good things about them.

"Hmm . . ." Matt flipped the page over—nothing—before racing out of the kitchen. "Look! This is weird." He found Frankie and Miguel still arguing over the cheese. He flashed the paper at them.

"Why am I on that?" Frankie asked, inspecting it. "And who is listening to me like this? That's my favorite thing to say."

"I don't know." Matt shrugged.

"It's so weird." Miguel scratched his head.

"What do you think it means?" Frankie asked. "Must be a clue. Something to lead us to another place."

"Maybe back into the kitchen?" Miguel pointed.

"It's a mess in there. I didn't see anything besides stuff

everywhere," Matt reported, going to hold the door open so they could see for themselves.

"Oh," Frankie replied. "I hate a dirty kitchen. You can't cook in a mess."

An idea jolted through Matt. He grabbed Frankie's arm. "Science!" he screamed.

Nacho cowered, tucking her face in Miguel's collar as he flinched. "Whoa!"

"What's wrong with you?" Frankie glared at him.

"Science! That's the answer." Matt started to walk toward the cafeteria doors.

"Where are you going? What does that mean?" Miguel replied.

"The labs. That's the clue. Look at Frankie's quote." He couldn't stop his feet from moving. The faster they got there, the faster he could get Ralphie back and out of this nightmare of a game.

Frankie and Miguel chased after him.

"We should tell the others." Miguel reached for the walkie-talkie clipped to Matt's hip, turning it back on. "Miguel to Becca."

They all inched into the hall.

"Hello?" Miguel shook it in the air.

"Danny here," came a voice on the other end.

"We have so much to tell you." Miguel rattled off

everything until he was out of breath.

"We have a lead, but we're still stuck in the gym," Danny said.

"Do you need us to come help you?" Miguel asked.

"No," Danny told him, sighing, "we're okay for now. No sense in us all getting trapped here."

"Got it," Miguel said. "Makes sense. Meet us as soon as you can."

CHAPTER 9

Ralphie on the Fritz!

Becca

"What *is* that?" Danny asked after signing off on the walkie-talkie. He stepped forward, his eyes scanning the intricate wall painting. The colors glowed in the darkness of the closet.

Becca stepped up near him to peer closer, taking in the lines, the sprawl, the eerie glow. "It looks like *another* map." She scratched her nose, curious, but she was also growing quickly tired of this whole thing.

Kylie pushed her way to the front of the group. "This is our way out!"

The map was drawn on the wall in front of them in careful intricate lines of glowing, neon ink. The ink was so bright, you could read it even in the dark. At the edge was an X that marked the spot and the label "Equipment Closet." From that spot, one distinct path slithered through the furniture pile they'd just dismantled.

Becca watched Kylie mumble to herself as she traced the paths and tried to unravel the puzzle. Kylie leaned closer again, squinting, like her eyes could zoom in like a telescope. "Danny, turn your camera light on, please."

Danny clicked on the bright light.

Kylie traced her fingers along the glowing paths and then pulled her hand back. "There are the two locker rooms, the bathrooms, and Coach Francisco's office. We have to go through there."

"But it's an office. . . ." Becca questioned, "How could it possibly take us out of the gym?" Part of her, deep down, hoped that maybe this at last was where her zoetrope was hidden. But her intuition told her this game was far from over.

"There's a second door," Danny replied. "It leads to the hall."

Becca had never known that. She'd never been in Coach's office for more than a minute, so she guessed she'd missed that.

"Have you ever wondered how he's able to catch you in the hallway between classes? Like he's always there quick with his whistle."

"Yeah," she said, even though she wasn't the type of kid to

be caught in the hall after the bell rang. Two Minutes Early Is Late was always her motto.

Kylie started to scratch at the wall.

"What are you doing?" Becca asked her.

"There's something taped to the wall and painted over. I can feel it." Kylie took Becca's hand and let her feel it, then waved Danny forward with the light as she scratched and clawed.

The girls yanked at it from both sides until it peeled off.

Kylie held up the silver-painted key.

"It has to be the key to Coach Francisco's office," Danny almost shouted. "Let's try it."

Becca nodded. "Sounds like a plan." She took the map from Matt's hands, and started carefully tracing the path with her finger, looking to Kylie for guidance. "Maybe you should lead the way."

Kylie nodded. "Okay, guys. Follow me." She led the way to Coach Francisco's office. It was sandwiched between the locker rooms. A sign read, "Keep out unless you need something—otherwise knock and wait!"

Kylie handed Becca the key. This had to work. It had to.

Becca slid the key into the lock and it turned with a click. They all gasped.

But now what? The office was completely dark—and eerie.

Danny turned on the camera light again. "Let me lead the way," he said, pushing through. "There should be a desk right around—OUCH!" Danny yelped as he slammed into a big wooden desk.

Becca rushed around and started opening the drawers, looking for the zoetrope. Just in case! She felt strange going through a teacher's office like this, like she was invading his privacy. She *hated* when her little sister, Katie, went through her stuff. But she needed to find Nana's heirloom, no matter what.

"I don't see anything," Kylie said.

"Me neither," Danny replied, still rubbing his elbow. He crossed the room, flashing light along each wall and crevice. But Danny didn't see the zoetrope anywhere.

"Same," Becca answered sadly. Maybe this was just the way out. Becca went over and stuck the key in the lock of the second door in the room, and they all sighed, relieved, when they heard the familiar click.

The whole group rushed forward, pushing through the door and into the hall.

They screeched to a halt.

Matt's robot stood there making strange noises.

"What's Ralphie doing here?" Becca asked, dropping to the floor, examining the robot, pushing buttons and pulling out random loose pieces.

Kylie called out Matt's name, wondering if the other group was nearby.

"Something's wrong," she said. "I think—"

Danny knelt down to examine Ralphie with her. "Yeah, this wasn't loose before, right?" He pulled another plug off the robot's tin chest.

Becca watched as Danny set the robot on the floor, clicking on and off the button that made it talk. Ralphie scooted across the floor, walking in stiff, robotic circles, like he was making himself dizzy. He was definitely making Becca dizzy, anyway.

Then the robot's eyes popped forward, and it started spinning around, confused. "I am a robot. My name is Ralphie." It paused, opening and closing its small metal jaw. Then it said a series of letters, repeating and shuffling them, over and over.

"X-O-R-B-A," it said, red eyes blinking every few seconds. "B-R-O-X-A! BROXA!"

Then it repeated the same phrase.

"What does this mean?" Kylie asked. She pulled out her notepad, scrawling it down.

"I don't know," Becca replied. "I bet Matt didn't program it to do that." She frowned. "Something's definitely wrong. He's going to freak out." Becca knew how much this robot meant to him, and if he didn't get on her nerves so badly, she would've halfway listened to all the things he'd told her about it when he visited her house with his mom.

"X-O-R-B-A," Ralphie said, blinking again. "BROXA!"

Becca repeated the word over and over again. What could it possibly mean?

"BROXA!"

"BROXA!"

"BROXA!"

The robot kicked its tiny silver feet and shouted the word over and over again as if that would help them understand.

What could the word mean? Was it even a word? It didn't seem like it. But maybe . . .

"It could be a clue," Becca said. "It has to be. Danny, get Matt on the walkie-talkie."

She shrugged, picking up Ralphie and holding him close. She examined him again, checking out the poor, confused robot from head to toe. And that's when she saw it.

A familiar logo sticker, right on the bottom of the robot's foot.

GM.

CHAPTER 10

Slimed!

Matt

Matt paced outside the science wing as they waited for Becca, Kylie, and Danny to get up here. What if the Game Master killed his robot? What if he broke it apart? What if he changed the programming? What if Ralphie was ruined?

His heart thudded. Becca had told him over the walkie-talkie that they'd found him. But she never said *how* they'd found him and what shape he was in.

"The Game Master," Miguel said, his voice low and worried. "He got to Ralphie?"

Matt nodded solemnly, afraid he might cry. But he held it together. He didn't like to cry. Though if he had to admit it, he cried more often than he'd like. But even so, he definitely didn't want them to see him cry. "Crying is a bridge to vulnerability," his mother always said when she'd catch him fighting away his feelings and turning red. He wasn't sure if he wanted to be "vulnerable" because he felt like that word really meant like X-ray vision. If a person saw you cry, then they'd be able to see your insides, the things that made you upset or sad . . . and maybe if you ever made them mad, they'd use those against you.

"He's going to be okay," Frankie said.

Matt wanted to believe them.

The sounds of footsteps echoed in the distance. Matt whipped around, spotting Kylie, Danny, and Becca racing down the hall.

Matt spotted Ralphie in Becca's arms. Intact. So far. His heart slowed.

"I got him." Becca held him out to Matt.

Matt grabbed him and held him to his chest. Ralphie repeated a phrase over and over again, but Matt's heart thumped so fast, that's the only sound he could hear. "You're okay," he whispered until the urge to cry disappeared.

"He keeps saying something," Kylie reported.

Matt gazed up at her. "What?"

"Ralphie's definitely a clue now," Kylie said, nodding to Matt.

Holding his camera up, Danny zoomed in on the robot's

foot, but Becca stepped forward, putting her hand over the lens. "Not Ralphie," she announced. "The letters. The letters Ralphie said—that's the clue."

"What?" Matt asked.

"He's been saying a word on repeat since we found him. Listen," Becca implored.

Everyone circled Matt. Ralphie started to talk again. Matt didn't know what was happening to Ralphie. He needed to get home and to his workshop. He'd use his tools to figure it all out. He would make sure his robot was okay.

"B-R-O-X-A!" Ralphie the robot announced again. "X-R-B-A-O!"

Everyone talked over one another as they tried to figure out what the letters meant. The chaos swirled around Matt like a storm. He closed his eyes and tried to focus. He needed to block out everyone's voices to think straight. What was Ralphie trying to tell them? "R-B-X-A-O!"

"Boar!" Frankie called out.

"Bora . . . like the place, maybe?" Becca said.

"Bra?" Miguel added, then giggled.

Kylie shot him a death glare. "That doesn't have all the letters!"

"Orb or oar, maybe?" Becca added.

"I think we need to use *all* the letters." Kylie glared some more.

"No, no, how about bro or boa?" Frankie added.

"Rob . . . like how the Game Master robbed you of Ralphie!" Danny shouted.

Matt frowned. "I'm just glad we found him." They needed to figure this out. But he still couldn't concentrate. His mind filled with all the bad things that could've happened to Ralphie. Becca stepped away, turning the letters over again and again in her head. Matt followed her, Ralphie in hand.

"R-X-O-B-A!" the robot declared.

He could see Becca's lips moving, arranging and rearranging the letters in her head. He remembered her doing that during their class reading time, too. She said it helped her think. Visualizing the letters in space moving around, connecting.

"B-R-O-X-A!" the robot said again.

"I got it!" Matt shouted. "I got it."

"X-A-R-O-B!" the robot said again.

"Borax!" Matt said. "B-O-R-A-X! Borax. That's it."

"What's borax?" Miguel asked as the snake slithered close, settling around his shoulders.

"It's a basic household chemical," Frankie declared smugly. "It's used in a lot of cleaning products."

"And where would one find borax in school?"

Frankie shrugged. "The science labs or the janitor's—"

But Matt didn't wait to listen. He raced toward the science lab. Becca chased after him, the whole group right on her heels.

Matt skidded to a stop in front of one of the science class-rooms. It was eerie and dark, glowing with a familiar green light. That had to be it. He pushed the door open. Becca followed him in, using her phone's flashlight to guide their path.

"Last one in make sure to hold the—" But Matt was too late. The lab door clicked behind them.

Danny tried the door. It would not budge. "Again?" he said, stamping his foot. "Again we're locked in? This is getting ridiculous."

Kylie nodded. "We should have known this would happen. Fool me once, or whatever."

Danny frowned, panning the room with his camera. "Yeah, but this is like the third time."

"We'll figure it out after the clue." Becca barreled ahead into the darkness.

Matt wished the window blinds weren't down and so dark, but sometimes the labs required darkness for experiments.

Frankie clicked on the overhead lights. The lab spread out before them, worktables covered with sheets and six cupcakes lined up on the front lab table. "Whoa," they said. "Those look great."

"Freeze!" Becca said as Frankie lifted one of the blue-and-red frosted cupcakes. "It could be like *Alice in Wonderland*."

"What?" Matt asked, almost wanting to laugh, even though this game wasn't the least bit funny yet.

"You know . . . the 'Eat Me'!" she pressed, quickly recounting the story of *Alice in Wonderland*. "It could have something in it."

"Not something that will make us grow ten feet tall," Kylie replied. "Right?"

Danny sucked his teeth and videoed every cupcake. "I'll have the evidence if we get food poisoning."

Matt heard Miguel's stomach growl beside him. He was getting hungry, too. It was almost noon, their usual dismissal time, but still it felt like they'd been here for a thousand years.

"We should just focus," Becca said.

"Your brain needs food to focus. Mrs. Gupta always says that. She makes breakfast part of homework," Miguel reminded, reaching for one.

"I don't know about this," Becca cautioned.

"We saw the supplies." Matt remembered the mess in the kitchens. That must've been for these cupcakes. Game Master cupcakes. When did food become part of an escape room?

"Where?" Becca's brow furrowed.

"The kitchens," Frankie said. "It was a mess in there. A real chef never leaves a messy kitchen. Ever. Well, they shouldn't. I won't."

"Okay," Becca replied. "I still don't think we should try them yet. Can we focus on the borax clue first? Then figure out what to do with the cupcakes."

Everyone grumbled but agreed. They headed toward the

shelves in the back, where the science teachers kept all the chemicals.

Matt and Becca got to work combing through the shelves of chemicals, looking for borax.

The loudspeaker crackled with static and that same deadpan, familiar voice. "Tick, tick, tick," it said. "You're running out of time. You're not paying attention. Better find what you need, or you'll lose the game—and your beloved zoetrope, too!" The voice crackled again and then disappeared.

"Dude," Miguel said, rolling his eyes as Nacho slithered forward, full of judgment. "The Game Master is scary." He hovered close to Becca, eyeing the chemicals. "Did you find the borax yet?"

Matt frowned. "Nothing. Not a single bottle. Or jar? Is it liquid?"

"What does borax even look like?" Miguel pulled out his phone. "Oh, right. Phones don't work."

The overhead speaker crackled again with that familiar, annoying tick-tick-tick, like it was mocking them all.

Frankie darted to the left of the classroom, grabbing at the sheets covering the tables. Underneath were textbooks and buckets of tools and goggles and lab coats.

"What are you doing?" Matt asked.

"Found it!" Frankie grinned.

Under the last sheet was a big piece of butcher paper, with a bunch of ingredients laid out on top: borax, glue, water, shaving cream, contact lens solution, and food coloring. Everyone stared at everything.

Matt examined all the bottles of random stuff. Contact solution. That borax powder.

"Looks like a science experiment," Frankie told him.

"But what are we supposed to do with it all?" Becca asked.

"Slime," Frankie declared as if it were the most obvious thing ever. "We're supposed to make slime. It's not exactly a *MasterChef*-worthy challenge."

Matt's jaw dropped. "But why?" he wondered out loud.

Frankie shrugged. "Don't know, don't care. But that's what it is. I made it with my sister. Bright purple. My mom made us toss it, though. She thinks it makes a mess."

Kylie turned to Frankie, looking them straight in the eye. "Then you know how to make it?"

Frankie grinned. "You bet I do!"

Kylie nodded. "Then get to it. Because I'm pretty sure this is a clue."

CHAPTER 11

Invisible Messages

Becca

Danny started the camera rolling as Frankie got to work. First, Frankie snatched Mrs. Parker's lab coat, then they affixed goggles to their eyes. Then they got out a bunch of beakers and test tubes and began ordering Matt around like he was their assistant. Together, Matt and Frankie carefully measured out the borax, glue, shaving cream, and contact lens solution.

And then, Frankie sat on the stool for a long moment, staring at the tiny bottles of food coloring. Red, yellow, blue, green.

Becca leaned in close, curious. Confused. "What are you doing?" she finally asked. "And when did you become *into* science?"

"Cooking is just one big science experiment," Frankie scoffed, then turned back to the task at hand. "Deciding the color," they said, and waved Becca away. "Give me a minute. It'll come to me."

Becca joined Kylie in pacing around the lab table impatiently. Kylie looked like she might just jump on Frankie if it motivated them to move faster.

"It's only been ten minutes," Becca reminded her.

"Eleven." Kylie crossed her arms over her chest. "How long does it take to make slime?"

"They're a chef. I guess chefs want everything perfect...," Becca whispered, which she completely understood. She was the same way about gymnastics. "Practice makes better," her mom always said, but Becca truly believed that practice makes perfect.

Kylie smiled.

Becca winked. No one wanted to hear Frankie start complaining again or delay them from getting to the bottom of this clue. "Come on." She gathered the rest of the crew while Frankie continued to work and Danny filmed them.

"I wonder if there are fingerprints on these." Danny held up the food coloring and tried to zoom in as close as possible.

"Unless your camera has infrared, you won't be able to see anything," Matt said.

"My camera is the best one on the market. That's what my dad said when he gave it to me."

"C'mon, guys. Focus. Why do you think the Game Master is making us make slime?" Miguel interrupted.

They all said their theories. Maybe they have to use the slime for something else. Maybe the slime itself was a clue. Maybe the process was the clue. They couldn't seem to decide.

"Well, let's try to be useful while Frankie and Matt are working," Miguel said. "Let's look for the zoetrope. It could be here somewhere."

Becca and the rest of the crew combed through the science lab, then went to the sliding glass door that separated the lab from the actual classroom.

"Danny, come on," Kylie said, pushing the step stool to prop the door open behind her. "We can check out this side of the room. Use your camera light to guide us until I can flip the switch and turn on the light."

Danny nodded, heading off after them.

"Matt, help me," Frankie called out.

Matt turned back to help and tripped over the step stool, knocking it over and letting the door slide shut behind him with a click.

Uh-oh!

Becca whipped around and watched as Matt scrambled to his feet and tried to slide the door back open. It was locked. He banged, tugged, and kicked at the door. Becca rushed back and shook the door from the other side. She shouted through the glass, "What happened?"

Everyone rushed to join her at the door and to watch a frantic Matt talk to Frankie. Their voices echoed and reverberated against the glass.

"I tripped over the stool and the door slid shut!" Matt shouted back. "Frankie, I'm sorry." He still tugged at the knob. "But I think we're stuck here, by ourselves."

Frankie looked up from all the mixing. "What are you—? Wait, why are they on the classroom side?"

Matt shrugged. "To look for the zoetrope."

Frankie abandoned the slime and strode past Matt. He grabbed the door handle again and Becca watched how they tried, too. Nothing. It was sealed tight as a drum.

They were good and stuck. Separated from the group.

"What do we do?" Frankie asked through the glass to Becca.

She rested her forehead against the glass, exasperated. "Finish the slime. See what's there. We'll keep going to see if there's another way out."

"Let's decide on a color," Matt said, his voice squeaking. He cleared his throat. "We need to finish making the slime. It's got to be a clue."

"I haven't figured out the colors," Frankie told the group.

"Who cares about colors?" Miguel shouted.

"It could be a clue." Frankie shrugged. "And the colors I have here are just so . . . basic."

Matt bit his lip. "We could try mixing?" he suggested. "You know, like yellow and blue."

Frankie frowned. "We already have green."

Matt grinned. "Red and blue?"

"Purple? Like last time. Why not?" Frankie shrugged.

"Just get it done!" Becca shouted, peering in through the glass walls of the science lab. "Bring the materials to the table that's closer to us so we can all see."

Danny pressed his camera to the glass. Kylie wiped smudges off.

Matt and Frankie darted back to the lab table and gathered everything. They brought it to the table closest to the door. Becca had a good view of everything now.

Something boomed.

Becca whipped around.

Kylie stood in the middle of a mess as it poured from the shelf. She tried to catch all the items tumbling down but couldn't. "Whoops!"

"What are you doing?" Becca asked. She tried to keep the irritation from her voice. She really wanted—*needed* everyone to focus so they could find the zoetrope and get the heck out of there.

Kylie's cheeks flushed and she pushed her black hair away from her face, then held out a glossy piece of paper. "It has Danny's name on it!"

"Me?" Danny jumped.

"Yeah, it's weird." Kylie cleared her throat and read out a list.

WHO IS DANNY WATSON?
"The camera can show you things that others can't see!"
1. Camera
2. Photography
3. Filmmaking
4. Movies and TV
5. Sour gummies!

Kylie flashed the paper at the group. "The paper is weird."

Danny's eyes opened super wide as he spotted his picture. He reached for it. "Why . . . what is this? Weird. It's photography paper. Like what pictures are printed on."

Becca knocked on the glass door, then grabbed Danny. "Show Matt and Frankie."

Danny pressed the glossy page on the wall. Frankie looked up.

"OMG!" Matt yelled. He plucked a folded piece of paper from Frankie's back pocket and raced to the glass. "Look!"

Becca's eyes scanned the page. Another one of these Wanted pages. But with things about Frankie. Weird. What was this all about?

Frankie turned back to the ingredients, continuing to pour and mix and shake. Precise and even.

"Why does Frankie always take forever?" Miguel complained.

"They're a chef," Danny replied. "Can't rush perfection."

Matt and Frankie squabbled as Matt, eager to help, knocked over a whole beaker of contact solution, spilling it all over the paper. Becca watched through the glass, her heart racing.

That's when Becca saw them.

Letters.

Forming quietly but clearly across the butcher paper.

Another clue.

Becca knocked on the glass. "Do you guys see that?" She pulled at the doorknob, forgetting that it was locked. "Look!" she said, jumping up and down and pointing. "Look, look, look."

"Oh my god, oh my god . . . it's a message," Danny said,

the sound of his camera zoom echoing.

Frankie looked down at the table, annoyed. "Great. Thanks, Matt. What a mess. Now I've got to remeasure the contact—" Then they saw them, too. The letters.

So did Matt. "It's another clue," he said.

"You're right," Frankie said, and looked at the ingredients for a moment before taking the bottle of contact solution and squirting it all the way across the table, soaking every inch of butcher paper. More and more letters appeared, fast and furious.

What goes up and comes down but isn't very smart and might deliver you a pizza at a restaurant?

But the letters quickly disappeared.

"Oh no!" Matt said.

"Wait!" Frankie took the wet and soggy slime and squished it on the paper, allowing the letters to show again.

"A riddle," Frankie said to the crew, staring at the sentences.

"What does it say?" Becca called out.

Kylie took her trusty notebook from her back pocket. "I'll write it down."

Frankie cleared their throat and reread aloud so Kylie could transcribe it.

"Great! Show it to me!" Becca shouted through the plate-glass wall. "We can try to solve it, too." The others had gathered as Frankie held up the paper. They were all puzzled.

"What goes up and down?" Danny asked.

"A ball?" Miguel said.

"Hmmm . . ." Kylie pursed her lips. "A rock?"

"People throw rocks and balls, but I think it's an elevator," Danny said.

"Elevators can work on their own, so they aren't 'dumb'!" Matt shouted through the glass windows.

"What delivers a pizza?" Becca asked herself.

"A pizza delivery man," Frankie replied.

"Yeah, duh, but not in a restaurant. They go to people's houses." Danny set his camera on the ground. "But a waiter gives you a pizza in a restaurant."

"*Waiter*," Becca said aloud. "I guess that might be part of this. But what does it mean?"

Matt tapped the paper. "What's not smart, though? Waiters are smart. They have to remember orders and stuff."

"A dumb waiter would be terrible," Kylie said. "And isn't 'dumb' a bad word to say? That's what Principal Collins says."

"Whatever." Matt rolled his eyes. "Why would this clue be a dumb waiter? This makes no sense."

Danny laughed again. "That just sounds silly."

"Wait, no," Becca said, and repeated the phrase over and over. "You're right. I've heard that before."

"It's a real word," Frankie said, shouting through the glass. "D-U-M-B-W-A-I-T-E-R. Dumbwaiter."

Matt shrugged. "I don't think that's true."

"No, it is. Back in the olden days, restaurants and hotels used it like a little service elevator. For food and stuff. So they wouldn't have to carry things up and down the stairs all the time. Back when kitchens were mostly underground, like the basement kitchen here." Frankie tapped their mouth for a moment. "I think the school has a dumbwaiter. At the end of the hall. Leading to the cafeteria. They cover it up, though. You guys have to go check it out. That's what the clue is telling us. Has to be."

"But what about the page about Danny? Do we think that's a clue, too?" Miguel asked. "I feel like it's trying to tell us something. Like when Matt found the one in the cafeteria kitchen, we knew to go to the labs. What do you think the clues are on Danny's page?"

"Hmm . . ." Becca started to pace and think. She looked at the page again. But what did photography and videos have to do with anything? She was having trouble thinking through everything. "I think we need to figure out the dumbwaiter first."

"I think we should try to do both," Kylie said.

Matt thumped the glass. "And get us out." He shrugged. Right.

All three things.

Becca turned to the others. "Okay, let's check out both," she said, trying to be the voice of reason. Her zoetrope was still missing, and all this back-and-forth was getting them nowhere. "In the meantime, Frankie and Matt, look for another key. There has to be one." She started to step away, then came back. "Danny, you stay behind and help. And figure out what your page"—she held it up—"has to do with everything."

Danny nodded. "Aye-aye, captain," he declared.

"We'll come back for you guys," Becca said. Frankie nodded. "Promise."

"Call us on the walkie-talkies," she said before leading the way down the hall with Kylie and Miguel right behind her.

The hall was dark and eerie; all the windows were covered with paper and lined with painter's tape. Buckets of paint and tarps lined the walls. Half the lockers had a fresh coat and the left side of the wall was a bright Hidden Vista blue.

Becca went straight to the place Frankie had mentioned and there it was: a small metal door with a handle, about three feet off the ground.

"Hmmm," Miguel said. "Never noticed that before."

"Me neither," Kylie added. "It's—it's kind of creepy, huh?"

Becca was intrigued. She stepped closer, pulling the handle. It made an eerie, screeching sound.

Miguel panned his phone and its light toward it, and the glow filled the space. They all stared at the screen, nervous about what they'd see. But it was a flat little cube of space and what looked like a wooden tray inside, slung up on a pulley made of ropes.

"Definitely weird," Miguel declared, shivering as Nacho slithered more tightly around his shoulders.

"The perfect place to maybe hide a zoetrope," Becca said, stepping closer. "Kylie, gimme some more light."

Kylie stepped closer, too, and Becca peered into the little space. She tugged at the small rope. It was a long way down.

Miguel waved his arms, frantic, scaring Nacho. "Uh, look around, guys. You sure we should do this?" He sighed deeply. "There's this creepy disembodied voice playing pranks and destroying robots. And now what? We're supposed to get in that thing?" His voice squeaked as he panicked.

"That's why we've got to do what we can to get out of here." Becca tugged the rope again.

Miguel swallowed hard.

"Get Matt on the walkie-talkie." She handed the device to Miguel.

"Miguel to Matt," he said.

"Matt here," came a voice on the other end.

"We found the dumbwaiter," Miguel said. "It actually exists. Tell Frankie."

"Told *you*," Frankie shouted.

"We'll see where this leads and also look for the janitor's keys to get you out of there," Becca said, determined.

"Matt's trying to pick the lock," Frankie replied. "And Danny is looking for a key to the sliding door."

"Good luck. We'll report back," Becca said before signing off.

Everyone stared back at the dumbwaiter.

Miguel frowned. "For the record, I don't think this is a good idea," he said.

"But we're going to try it anyway," Becca said as she climbed inside. "Wish me luck."

CHAPTER 12

Calls and Cupcakes

Matt

Matt tried the door to the hallway again while Frankie tried the sliding one from the lab to the classroom. But it wouldn't budge.

"Ugh!" Matt shouted. The frustration was bubbling up in him and he was afraid he'd be boiling over any second now. His dad *hated* when Matt lost his cool. He'd always say that anger made it impossible to think and clogged your brain cells. But Matt really wanted to throw something right now.

Frankie retreated, too, heading back to the front desk. "I'm so over this." They thumped at the cupcakes, flicking frosting angrily in several directions.

Danny slumped on the other side of the glass door, taking

a break. Matt watched him plug in his camera and stare at the paper with his name on it. Matt heard him mutter, "This sucks," over and over.

"Who do you think it is?" Matt asked.

"I don't care." Frankie sat, frustrated, and stared at the wall.

"What about you?" Matt yelled in Danny's direction, hoping his voice carried.

Danny shrugged, his hair pressed up against the glass like a dark pancake. He held up the page about him, and Matt could see some of the things. "I think that Becca, Kylie, and Miguel went to the wrong place," Danny admitted.

"Then what's the clue?" Frankie asked, finally succumbing to the look of the cupcakes and shoving one in their mouth.

"Not sure, but I feel like the clue you all got last time was to come up here. That was from the page you found in the kitchen."

Frankie nodded with cheeks full of cupcake. They finished the cupcake in one huge bite.

"Then where would we go based on the list about you?" Matt asked, jumping to his feet and going closer to the glass door.

"Hmm . . ." Danny read the list out loud again. "The art room, maybe? That's where the darkroom is."

"The darkroom?" Matt scratched his head.

"Like where you develop photographs. There's also a small theater in there, too, where Mrs. Calhoun lets us play our films." Danny shook that paper. "Yeah, that's what I think the clue is."

Matt felt like Danny was right. The Game Master was playing two games with them. Leading them this way *and* that way. Matt didn't know why . . . but he felt sure there were two games they were playing. Now, if only they could get out of this room and get to the art room.

Matt grabbed the walkie-talkie off the table and pressed the button. "Matt to Becca."

"Miguel here," came a voice. "What's up?"

"Danny thinks that we need to go to the art room next," he reported.

"Why?"

"Based on the list about him. He thinks it's important."

"Okay. Well, Becca's headed down the dumbwaiter. We'll see what's up with that, too, and meet you there. Ummm . . . did you get out?"

Matt sighed. "Not yet but—"

Frankie started to cough. They spit out most of the cupcake they'd consumed onto the floor.

"What's happening?" Miguel's voice held concern.

"Gotta go!" Matt raced over to Frankie, who was now red and sweating and coughing. Danny banged on the door and pressed his brown cheeks to it.

Matt patted Frankie on the back, trying to help them to stop choking.

A bright silver object shot from their mouth.

Frankie lay flat on the floor, panting in relief.

"You okay?" Matt asked as he went to retrieve the object.

"Yeah," Frankie replied, out of breath. "There was something in that cupcake."

Danny yelled through the glass and Frankie tried to assure him.

Matt leaned down and picked up the slimy, frosting-covered object. He spotted tiny silver grooves. He went to the science lab sink to rinse it off.

"What is it?" Frankie asked, peeling themself off the floor.

"It's a key!" Matt held it up. "And I bet it's the one we need."

Frankie grabbed the cupcake wrapper. "It has words on it. Ones I didn't notice before. It says, 'Freedom is sweet!'"

Matt raced to the glass door and tried the key. Bingo!

The door opened. Danny rushed in. Then, Matt went to the classroom door and tried it there. Another success!

They were free.

CHAPTER 13

Dumbwaiters Are Scary

Becca

The dumbwaiter felt even darker than the hallway, but Becca was trying to swallow her nerves as she sat in the weird metal box. They were all tired, cranky, and hungry and she couldn't stand to play this game for much longer. This had to end. Now. And she would end it. No matter what it took.

Climbing into the little space that held the dumbwaiter had seemed like a smart idea a few moments ago. But being in there now, Becca worried. The thing was clearly old and rickety, and who knew how much weight the ropes could actually hold? But every other door was locked, every window sealed shut. They'd be stuck on the science floor forever if they didn't do something. This was the only way out. As she sat on the cold metal slab and peered up, Becca turned on her phone light, flashing bright in Kylie's eyes.

"You ready?" she asked.

Kylie raised her hand to shield her eyes and Becca lowered her phone. "As ready as I'll ever be." She gulped.

Kylie tugged the dumbwaiter door open another inch or two. It made a creepy creaking noise. Becca figured it must have been years since the last time someone opened it. Kylie reached up for the pulley ropes. "I still don't think this is a smart idea," she said, again.

"Yeah," Miguel said with a snort. "It's dumbwaiter. Get it, *dumb*waiter?" He laughed to himself.

"It's the only shot we've got," Becca announced, trying not to sound bossy. People were always calling her bossy. But she wasn't. She just had leadership skills. And right now, let's be honest, they really needed leadership skills. Someone had to take charge.

She looked at her ragtag crew. Miguel was silly and distracted. Kylie was smart and generally useful, but she was starting to get on Becca's nerves with all the negativity. Frankie, Matt, and Danny were back in the science lab. Probably with Matt focused on Ralphie and Frankie eating those cupcakes. Danny was always so busy staring through the camera lens, focusing on shots, that he often missed the big picture. Becca knew her thoughts were spiraling now because she was hungry. Her blood sugar was dropping. She felt a bit wobbly—like at gymnastics practice when they ran out of granola bars. Which she had in her bag. Which was still in homeroom. If they got back there, Becca would share. They all had to be starving by now.

She shook her head, trying to regain her focus. She could almost hear in her head the Game Master's taunting, ticking clock.

Actually, they could all hear it. Because there it was again, over the crackling static of the loudspeaker. "Tick, tick, tick," the Game Master's annoying voice chimed through. "Time to get a move on. Are you dumb enough to try?"

They all stared at each other, frozen.

"That was definitely a clue," Kylie said, her eyes wide.

"Yeah," Danny said, swallowing hard. "But 'dumb enough to try'?"

"Or we shouldn't try!" Miguel added. "I vote for nope. Nope. Nope. Nope."

"We have to," Becca said. This was all her fault. The Game Master had her nana's zoetrope. It was on her to get it back and to get them all out safely. No matter what it took. "Whatever you do," she warned, "don't let the dumbwaiter door close." They'd been locked out—locked in?—too many times already.

Kylie pulled out the walkie-talkie. "I'll tell Matt, Danny, and Frankie." She pressed the red button. "Matt, Frankie, Danny. You guys! Roger, one-two-three. I heard that on TV," she informed the group. "Come in. Come in."

The walkie-talkie crackled with noise but no voices.

"I'll keep trying them," Kylie said.

"Let's do this!" Becca took a deep breath. The dumbwaiter was dark and rickety. She wasn't sure it could hold her weight. But now she was in the little space, sitting on the small metal surface, her hands gripping the ropes. Using the light on her phone, she took a deep breath, and got to work. She pulled it in one direction, hoping it would start her descent. But the dumbwaiter wouldn't budge. Then she tugged it the other way. For a moment, nothing happened. But as she tugged harder, the base started to rise.

"OMG! You're going up!" Kylie called out.

"Looks that way," Becca shouted back.

Don't be afraid.

Don't be afraid.

Don't be afraid.

Slowly, slowly, slowly . . . for what seemed like forever, Becca pulled and shifted, pulled and shifted, adjusting her weight to balance on the cold metal beneath her. She was dripping in sweat by the time she finally made it to what seemed like another door. There was no handle. Just a small metal cutout. But she was starting to feel cramped, claustrophobic. So she shoved it hard. And thankfully, it flung open.

She scrambled out of the small space, hitting the ground with a hard thud.

She waited for her eyes to adjust, taking in the darkness, the shadows. There was a poster half-torn on the floor beside her. She knew this poster. She was in the algebra room, on the far end of the math wing. The back wall of the classroom was covered with posters of different equations, and when she'd opened the dumbwaiter door, she'd ripped right through one.

"You okay?" Kylie's voice called from the darkness of the dumbwaiter.

"Yeah! I'm out!" Becca shouted down into it. "I think I'm on the third floor. In the algebra class."

She heard Miguel groan. He didn't love math either.

Becca flashed her phone light through the space, her eyes making out shapes in the darkness. And there, that familiar sight. A path of stickers—the GM symbol glowing green and sinister in the dark. But it wasn't just the path. The stickers were everywhere, on the walls, on the floor, covering all the spaces.

Becca sighed. Tired. Then she shouted down to the others, "Come on up, guys! It's not over yet!"

CHAPTER 14

Phone Calls!

Matt

Matt darted through the science halls with Danny and Frankie on his heels. They headed for the staircase. Matt tried to talk to Kylie through the walkie-talkie while running but he could barely get his words out.

"We . . . think . . . you're . . . going . . . to . . . the . . . wrong . . . place!" he shouted as they leaped up three stairs at a time.

But before he could wait for Kylie's response, there was a loud SPLAT!

Frankie hesitated on the steps, but Danny couldn't stop midjump and neither could Matt. They crashed together in a pile of limbs at the end of the hall, elbows in Matt's ribs, a knee in his back. "Whoa. Why'd you stop short?" he asked.

"Did you hear that?" Frankie cowered.

"I heard it, too." Danny inched forward to gaze up the set of stairs.

Matt stood and dusted himself off, annoyed, then aimed his phone's light up into the staircase. There was nothing. Empty. He turned back to Frankie and Danny, ready to call them scaredy-cats. "There's—"

SPLAT!

Matt leaped out of the way before a balloon crashed down, splattering paint all over the floor and him.

"What the— Who's up there?" he screamed.

Another balloon fell, this one filled with dirt. And another filled with water.

"Run!" Frankie shouted, jumping to their feet.

The balloons rained down, bursting with all kinds of things as the kids darted in the opposite direction.

They leaped down the stairs and slid on the banisters, desperate to get to the bottom floor. The balloons didn't stop coming. One caught Frankie on the back. Bright yellow paint. Another crashed into Danny's shoulder—luckily not the one where his camera sat—and covered him with a sticky goo. Matt barely got off easy with an ice-cold one straight to the face.

They slipped and slid their way off the staircase and into the hallway.

"What the heck was that?" Matt screamed as they bolted around the corner.

Frankie stopped to catch their breath, but Danny pushed them forward. "Keep going. I think they're behind us."

Matt's legs felt like spaghetti. Sweat raced down his back and he thought his heart might vomit up and out of his chest. All he could hear were the sounds of their sneakers squeaking and pounding the linoleum. They just had to get away. A few more steps.

BOOM!

SPLAT!

The noise of more balloons bursting against the ground followed them.

Matt looked around for an open door. Danny tried each one. Nothing opened. They turned left down the main corridor: the one everyone called the Hall of Justice, where Vice Principal Pinter had his office. Pinter the Punisher. That was what everyone called him. He gave out detention for breathing—or even sneezing. If he'd said no talking and you made a sound . . . detention!

Matt didn't want to try the doorknob to his office but there was no other place to hide.

The door opened with a click.

"In here," Matt called out, almost yanking both Frankie and Danny inside.

He quickly closed the door behind them and turned the lock. They all sprawled out on the cool floor, tired limbs stretching this way and that way. Matt waited for his heart and breathing to slow down. He felt his pulse vibrate through him.

"Where are we?" Frankie asked, looking all around at the office.

"Mr. Pinter's," Matt grumbled. "How have you never been in here?"

"I don't get detention," they replied with confidence.

"We need to stay here for a beat," Danny said, plugging in his camera and lying flat on the floor. "I need a minute."

Matt looked around. It didn't feel the same. All of Mr. Pinter's annoying "Be a Better Student" charts and posters were missing from the walls. The containers with his torturous detention homework were absent from the long table.

Frankie nosed around the room. Matt knew Pinter would hate that, but he didn't say anything. Pinter was probably taking the summer off anyway. He'd never know who'd been in here.

"I found something." Frankie lifted up a huge piece of chart paper. It looked like a blueprint, a weird map of instructions for a building. "It says, 'Phase One.' What does that even mean?"

"It's the school," Danny said, his eyes scanning the plans. "This looks sort of like what me, Becca, and Kylie found in the gym."

It was drawn carefully by colored pencils and markers, the lines ruler straight, a scale for measurement.

"What is that?" Frankie asked, running their fingers over the different rooms.

Matt's eyes grew wide as he took in all the detailed plans. In the homeroom six little figures smiling, unsuspecting, each bearing one of their names; the Gupta code to get them out of the classroom; the gym and its map and game; Ralphie and all his commands; and even Becca's zoetrope, drawn right there in ink. All carefully plotted and planned. He couldn't believe someone had set all this up.

His brain buzzed with a thousand questions.

But why?

Who wanted a zoetrope?

Who wanted his robot?

Who wanted to torture them?

Who hated them that much?

"And look." Danny tapped the page and Frankie flipped it over. "There's a list! Another one."

WHO IS KYLIE DAO?
"A map can have a thousand destinations!"
  1. *Maps*
  2. *Traveling*
  3. *Camping*
  4. *Cartography*
  5. *Blueprints*

"Why would anybody make these? Like what do they have to do with anything?" Matt asked.

"It's like someone is trying to get to know us," Danny said, after grabbing his video camera and getting good footage of it. "Or something."

"But why?" Frankie asked.

Matt shrugged. "Maybe—"

The sound of heavy footsteps echoed outside the door. Matt, Frankie, and Danny ducked beside the desk. A hooded figure appeared in the window.

Frankie gasped. Matt clasped a hand over their mouth. He spotted all the sweat beads across Danny's brown forehead. "Don't move," he whispered hard.

The person outside the door spoke to someone. Matt craned to listen.

"Yes, they're still here," said the garbled voice. "They are putting it all together as planned."

The hairs on Matt's arms rose. Whose voice was that? It

sounded robotic, like the voice files he had listened to while picking the perfect voice for Ralphie. That wasn't a *real* voice.

"Yes, yes," the voice said again. "They will be summer schooled indeed."

Matt looked at Frankie and Danny and gulped.

What did that mean?

CHAPTER 15

Up, Up, and Not Quite Away

Becca

Slowly, slowly, slowly, Kylie and Miguel—plus Nacho—pulled their way up in the dumbwaiter. It felt like forever for each of them to make the trip up. Becca waited, tapping her feet, trying hard not to nibble her nails. She tried to solve a random math problem in her head. But it just made her brain hurt. Or maybe that was hunger.

"I can't get Frankie or Danny or Matt on the walkie-talkie," Kylie said again for the fifth time as she looked around the room, frowning. "They aren't answering."

"Let's give it a couple minutes. Something's got to be happening," Becca said, hoping that something was finally something good.

Becca waved at all the stickers covering every visible surface.

"Definitely a clue," Miguel said as Nacho slithered close. "But what could it mean? There's no pattern to it all that I can see."

Becca walked the room, flashing her phone light, trying to figure out if the stickers on the floor might actually mark a path. They led down one side toward the door to the classroom, ending abruptly in front of it. The other kids followed as she grabbed the doorknob and gave it a tug.

But of course it didn't open.

Miguel sighed, then flipped the light switch, and the lights flickered on. "Sweet," Miguel said, pumping his fist a beat before a red liquid poured down from the ceiling, thick and steaming all over the floor. "Wait. . . . What is happening?"

He tried to duck out of the way but was too late.

It looked like . . .

"Blood!" Becca shouted.

"Yikes!" Kylie called, backing away.

Becca tried to stay calm.

Miguel stepped forward to try to help, but he lost his footing, slipped, and landed butt first right in the red mess.

"You okay?" Becca shouted, rushing forward to help him.

Nacho slithered down into the pools of red. She wasn't afraid. She even licked it with her forked pink tongue.

"That's it. This is too much," Kylie said, taking deep breaths to calm herself as best she could. "We need to get out of here!"

"It's not blood," Miguel said, dipping a finger into the mess and taking a lick.

The girls grimaced in horror.

"It's . . ." He pondered for a moment. "It's corn syrup. Nacho loves sweets."

Becca laughed, grateful that it wasn't actually blood. "Yeah, now that I take a closer look, it's too red," she said. "My mom is a nurse. Real blood is darker, and thicker."

"Well, whatever it is," Miguel said, taking a lick, "I'm covered in it."

Kylie felt bad for Miguel, but she was also trying to be careful not to get more syrup on herself.

That's when they spotted them. Right there on the floor where Miguel had crash-landed.

Becca stepped closer, careful to avoid the mess. But there they were, those pieces: pentominoes. The little block things made out of cubes. Five cubes. They played with them in math class. Made interesting shapes out of them. Becca didn't quite get why. But they were fun.

She stared down at them. Why were they here, lying in a fake pool of blood?

Kylie found a stash of wet wipes and helped Miguel clean himself up.

Becca tried to focus on the pentominoes. They had to put them back in the math widget basket after using them in class. No math teacher would ever leave them out like this. They must be important.

The door slammed. Loud. Dramatic. Unprompted. Apparently, all by itself.

Becca jumped.

A sticky Miguel looked up. "What happened?"

Kylie rushed over to it, but Becca already knew. It was definitely, decidedly locked. Again. They were stuck inside a math room filled with fake blood. Someone had slammed it from the outside. The only way out was the dumbwaiter.

Kylie sighed, all dramatic. "I'll go, then," she said. "We've got to keep moving. We can't stay here."

She headed toward the back wall, opened up the creaky metal door, and tried to pull the ropes. But they were jammed.

"It's not budging," she said, panic creeping into her voice. "It's stuck, too. Something heavy is down there holding it." She peered into the darkness, swallowing hard.

"Let me try," Miguel said, using his still-sticky hands to grip the ropes. But Kylie was right. They would not budge.

"Guess that's out," Kylie said with a shrug. She turned on her phone light to try to see down the long shaft.

Becca plopped down, defeated, sticky syrup coating her legs. "Now what?" she said. But no one answered.

They were trapped.

Again.

Darkrooms and Clues

Matt

Matt eased open Vice Principal Pinter's door and checked to see that the coast was clear. He, Frankie, and Danny darted up the staircase to the fourth floor. It was the obvious way to go.

Matt got to come up to the fourth floor only once a week for art classes. Otherwise it was for the eighth graders only. He loved coming up here every chance he got. Big skylights overhead made the rainbow-colored lockers shimmer in the sun. There was a large open patio off one end of the hall, perfect for warm-weather lunch breaks. And there was even access to a rooftop garden, though most of them had never gotten to see it. Again, eighth-grade privileges only. He couldn't wait until it was *his* turn.

The loudspeaker cackled with that familiar static, always a warning, and then there was a voice. "Tick-tock, tick-tock," it taunted again. "Better watch the clock. Your time is about to run out."

The kids paused, panicked, then looked around, frantic.

"The art room is this way!" Danny shouted, leading the way.

"Faster!" Frankie called out. "I don't want to get caught."

Their sneaker squeaks echoed through the hall as they turned left and right, then left again into the art corridor. Murals covered the walls and the hall still smelled of Mrs. O'Connell's kiln and tempera paints. Three large studios lined one side and a student lounge sat on the other.

Matt's pulse raced with every footstep. This was it. This had to be the last challenge. How much longer could this be? Matt felt like this was where the zoetrope had to be. There was no place left to go. All they had to do was find it and then find a way to get the heck out of here. It was time to escape this school.

Danny held the art room door open.

"My camera needs to charge again." Danny searched for an electrical socket. "The battery is really old. Let's go into the darkroom. We'll be safe in there—and I can show you how a darkroom works."

"How do you know all this stuff?" Matt asked.

"My mom's a filmmaker and my dad's an amateur photographer. Our house is basically one big film studio and darkroom. Well, at least the basement is." Danny grinned.

"Cool," Frankie replied. "That's why you're so good at this. I guess it's the same as my grandma teaching me how to bake."

Danny nodded and led the way to the back of the classroom, where the door read, Darkroom and the warning:

CLOSE THE DOOR BEHIND YOU! DON'T RUIN THE PHOTOS!

"I help Mrs. O'Connell clean up the art room every Friday," Danny boasted as he opened the room and clicked on the light.

Matt thought it couldn't even be called a light. A tiny hum echoed through the room as a red glow came from the ceiling. "It's way dark in here."

"You can't have too much light or the photographs won't develop," he said.

Long ropes crisscrossed over their heads. Wooden clothespins sat on the lines. A cabinet held solutions and supplies, and a table was stacked with paper. Matt didn't know anything about how pictures were made. He thought you took one on your phone or a camera and it ended up printed. He guessed this was the old way of doing things.

"Now what?" Frankie asked. Danny walked to the center of the room where a table held an old camera.

Matt wandered around looking at everything. Mrs. O'Connell had black-and-white photos on the walls and instructions for developing all different kinds of film that he'd never heard of.

"The camera—there's a note on it that says, 'Come find the secrets I have to hide!'" Danny said. "I think I need to develop the film in it."

"You know how to do that?" Matt asked.

"You'll see." Danny cracked his knuckles and got to work. "You've got to use a film tank." Matt and Frankie watched in awe. He set up the workspace: gathered a timer, two containers, a thermometer, several bottles of liquid, scissors, and more. He reached high above them and plucked four clothespins from the lines.

Matt had no idea how any of these things went into developing film. Danny popped open the camera and took the film out. His hands moved lightning fast and Matt couldn't keep up. Danny put the film on a reel and then put it in a weird contraption, then he started to mix chemicals like Frankie had done earlier.

"Okay, we have to wait ten minutes," he said, setting his timer, then turning the film tank over and over in his hands. "Let's go through suspects while we wait. Who do you think the Game Master is?"

"I think it's Vice Principal Pinter," Matt blurted out. "He hates me."

"But he likes me," Frankie replied. "And why would he torture us like this?"

Matt thought maybe they were right. But he still didn't like Vice Principal Pinter.

"I think it's Mrs. Gupta," Danny said while shaking the canister in his hands. "She's probably still mad at us."

"But *this* mad?" Frankie asked. "To do all of this?"

"We—actually Matt gave her a hard time this summer," Danny said.

Matt didn't try to lie. He'd been the worst. He couldn't even deny it. This summer had been a tricky one. His parents had been fighting a lot and his dog, Rufus, had been sick. Every day he'd woken up and had to go to school instead of going to his workshop to play with Ralphie or experiment with even more things. He'd just been so frustrated. He knew he shouldn't have taken it out on Mrs. Gupta. He probably owed her one of those forgive-me cards his mom had sent out whenever he'd misbehaved in elementary school.

The timer dinged.

Danny took the film canister back to the table. He added more chemicals and even rinsed this thing and that thing in the room's sink. He took the photo papers out and hung them up.

"So what's going to happen now?" Frankie asked, gazing up.

"It'll develop. The pictures will show up," Danny said with triumph.

They watched and waited. The time seemed to stretch and feel like a thousand years had passed before dark streaks and splotches appeared on the papers. Matt squinted to see in the subtle darkness. He wondered what it would show. The picture on the right filled in the fastest.

Frankie got super close, their nose almost grazing the paper. "It's letters!"

Matt watched as the paper filled in. It almost felt like magic.

WHO IS MIGUEL CÓRDOVA?
"Nachos aren't just for eating!"
1. *His snake*
2. *Pets*
3. *Angelito*
4. *Future vet*
5. *Shorty Helper*

"Someone knows him really well," Frankie said.

They turned to the other page. It filled in slowly, like it knew they were watching and waiting.

Piece by piece, the colors filled in.

"I know what 'Shorty Helper' means!" Danny shouted,

jumping excitedly. "Shorty the Starling!"

"What?" Matt stared at him in shock

"You know. The school mascot. Shorty the Starling."

"Wait, Shorty is real?"

"Of course he's real," Danny said. "He lives in the aviary sanctuary on the roof of our school. You know, in the roof garden?"

"Oh," was all Frankie said. "You've been to the roof garden?"

"You haven't?" Danny took the pictures down and led them out of the darkroom. "Yeah, Miguel is one of Mr. Castro's helpers. Taking care of the animals. He told me about it last year. I even got to take pictures of Shorty for the school newspaper." He paused, grinning to himself. Then frowned. "That probably means—"

"We need to find Shorty!" Matt said.

CHAPTER 17

What's a Pentomino?

Becca

Kylie and Miguel kept tugging at the rope, hoping they'd magically be able to fix it. But it wouldn't move.

"Hey," Kylie said, shoving at Miguel angrily. "You're getting fake blood on my sleeve!"

"No fighting," Becca said, like she was scolding her siblings. "We need to work together."

But she couldn't find the energy to get up off the floor to break up their argument. She felt lost. Alone. Frustrated. This was getting harder and harder. Part of her wanted to give up and part of her wanted to scream.

She felt Miguel's eyes on her.

"Oh man," he said to Kylie. "I think something's up with Becca." They glanced over, watching her just sit. Silent. Like a creepy blond doll. There was fake blood all over her legs. And it was like she didn't even care.

"This is bad." Kylie rushed toward her. "Come on, Becca." She pulled her up by her arms. "Let's keep moving, like you said. We need to find your zoetrope and get out of here."

Becca blinked slowly once, twice, three times and she knew Kylie was trying to get her to rally and cheer up. Even though Kylie *hated* messes, Becca could tell she was willing to deal with the stickiness if it meant helping Becca get through this. She just felt so frustrated—but she really didn't want to cry. No one in this room had seen her cry before and she didn't want this to be the first time.

Kylie pulled out a wet wipe and handed it to Becca. "Let's get you cleaned up and figure this out," she said. "Then we can get out of here and get some lunch."

Maybe those were the magic words because Becca nodded, slowly, then smiled. "Yes, out of here. Lunch."

They quickly wiped away all traces of corn syrup, except for the bit that now coated Becca's left sneaker. There was no salvaging it, and her mother would not be happy. Then they started scanning the room, searching for clues, trying to figure out what exactly they might be looking for.

Miguel tried the door again, hopeful, but there was no movement. And the ropes on the dumbwaiter wouldn't budge either. He sighed.

Then out of nowhere, a bucket above the door fell to the floor. Miguel dived out of the way. The last of the fake blood oozed out. Miguel pushed it away, but a plastic baggie caught his eye. "Look!" He pulled it from the base of the bucket and wiped away the goo. "A sandwich bag. But it has something in it. A piece of paper." He quickly unfolded it.

Becca's heart thudded as she waited.

"It's another list." He flashed it at them and then read it aloud.

WHO IS MATT DAREY?
"A good prank is worth a hundred laughs!"
1. *Ralphie the robot*
2. *Pranks*
3. *Making people laugh*
4. *His prank lab/robot workshop*
5. *Has two brothers and a sister*

"Why is this person writing this weird stuff about us?" Kylie asked.

"I don't know." Becca thought for a long moment. These lists felt like answers to those questions your teachers had you fill out on the first day of school. What are your likes and dislikes? What are your favorite things to do? Hobbies? It felt like someone was taking an inventory about them and watching them. But who? She took a deep sigh. "It doesn't feel like a clue."

"I'll keep it just in case." Miguel folded it and slipped it into his pocket.

Everyone started looking around the classroom again. But as the seconds turned to minutes, everyone got frustrated.

"There's nothing here," Becca said, her voice sad and tired. "And the zoetrope is nowhere to be found. This was a trap. Maybe we'll be stuck here forever."

"No," Kylie said, peering into the shelves, behind the other math objects, looking for a clue. "We're here for a reason. The stickers prove as much." She shuddered. "And so do the buckets of fake blood."

Becca sat on the ground again, kicking one of the pentominoes. It flipped over. She peered closer at it.

"Do you see that?" Becca said.

Kylie grimaced, because now there was syrup on Becca's other sneaker, too. "At least they're a matched set," she said, trying her best to be positive.

"No, not my shoe," Becca said. Though Kylie was right. "The pentomino."

It didn't look quite the way it usually did during algebra class, not that Becca had spent all that much time analyzing pentominoes. There was something on the back: a number. She picked it up.

"Guys, look!" she called to Kylie and Miguel, who rushed

over. She showed them the pentomino. "Let's gather them all. This has to be a clue." They knelt in the fake blood and gathered all the pentominoes from throughout the room. "Let's put them together and see what happens."

"Wait," Miguel said as they stared at all the pieces, trying to figure out how to pull together the puzzle. "Ms. Ahmed showed us how they work." He demonstrated how each pentomino could make different shapes. "Pentominoes or polyominoes are plane shapes made by joining squares together," he continued, folding and unfolding one to demonstrate. "But these are numbered, so let's just arrange them instead of putting them together."

"I don't get it," Kylie said after they'd watched a third time. "What does it mean?"

"We've got to line them up," Miguel said, making a row of pentominoes. "Let's see what they arrange."

Becca nodded, excited. "Worth a try," she said, her voice rising with energy. "We can figure this out if we work together."

Kylie frowned. "How?"

"Watch!"

They worked quickly, all three of them together, flipping them over and arranging them by number. Some of the pentominoes were letter shaped. Some looked like an S and others a T, and more.

Once they were in numerical order, they all stared down

at it. "It's some sort of message," Becca said. "But what? The letters look weird."

"Some of the letters are upside down and sideways." Miguel adjusted some of the pieces.

Becca kneeled down in front of the squares, the stress building in her legs and shoulders.

Then there it was again, the crackle of the loudspeaker. That endless static. And then the familiar, terrifying tick-tock-tick-tock.

"I've got it!" Miguel said. "Had to turn some of the letters upright."

Becca jumped up.

Miguel stood above the pentominoes and read aloud:

"SHORTS FLY!"

"What does that mean?" Kylie said.

"I don't know," Miguel said as Nacho slithered through the pieces, licking up more syrup as he went.

"Hmm," Becca said, looking closely.

She stopped, staring at the pentomino message again.

"Shorts . . . shorts . . . hmmm . . . summer . . . People wear shorts. . . . . But shorts don't fly. . . . Hmmm . . ."

The walkie-talkie in Kylie's hand shrieked, startling everyone.

"You guys!" a voice called, frantic. "You guys, you there?" It was Frankie, their voice staticky and faraway.

"Kylie here," she said back.

"We figured out where to go next!" Frankie said.

"Where are you?"

"We went to the art room!" they replied. "And figured out the next location."

"Where is it?" Kylie said eagerly.

"The roof!"

Becca, Kylie, and Miguel exchanged a puzzled glance.

"Where Shorty the Starling is!"

"SHORTY!" Becca shouted.

"The mascot," Kylie replied.

"That's it!" Miguel exclaimed.

They all looked down at the pentominoes again. That was the answer to the riddle. Shorty, the school's mascot, lived on the roof in an aviary and all the kids at Hidden Vista Middle School called him either Shorts, Shorty, or Shortie Bird!

"Tell them what we found," Becca told Kylie.

But Kylie handed the walkie-talkie to Miguel. "You can explain it better."

"We are in the math room and there are those

131

pentominoes . . . you know the ones we had to use in math class?" Miguel explained how they had figured out they spelled, "Shorts Fly."

"Whoa!" came a reply from Frankie, Matt, and Danny.

"Only one problem." Miguel's face crumpled as he replied into the walkie-talkie. "We're trapped. You've got to come open the math room door from the outside."

"We're on our way!"

CHAPTER 18

Shorty Want a Zoetrope?

Matt

After freeing Becca, Kylie, and Miguel from the math room, Matt and his five friends took the elevator up to the roof. A large garden and glass greenhouse stretched out in front of them. Fat tomatoes grew on vines and plump watermelons pushed out of the soil. Peppers in every color sprouted from dozens of clay pots. A tiny cornfield created a natural fence between the garden and the aviary. There were endless rows of planters, each bursting with a different kind of fruit or vegetable: squash, cucumbers, carrots, even a peach tree, though there were no peaches. Vines of grapes climbed a large trellis that leaned against one brick wall. Stone pavers created paths between the different sections.

The kids stepped carefully in case the Game Master had planted traps along the paths between garden boxes.

At the center sat a large wrought cage, familiar, like the ones they'd seen in zoos. And from inside it, they heard loud squawking sounds. The aviary. And Shorty the Starling.

Matt took a deep breath. Becca took one, too. They had to be on the right path now. They had to be nearly done with this game. He could feel it in his bones, in the way his fingers and toes tingled.

"Over there!" Miguel said, leading the way. He stepped right up to the cage, peering inside, eye to eye with the creature they had been looking for.

Inside that cage sat Shorty the Starling, Hidden Vista Middle School's proud mascot. He was not tiny but also not large. Nearly all his features were black, but something glimmered in his plumage like light or jewels, nearly iridescent. Shorty was decidedly the most temperamental mascot in the history of mascots. The one that their science teacher Mr. Adisa said was protective and fussy, and if provoked, very aggressive.

They all stared in awe or perhaps horror, especially after all they'd been through. All those challenges. All that drama. This was where the game had led them.

Matt sighed, stepping forward. He knew this was it. The last challenge before they could get out of here.

Becca peered into the cage, looking at the bird. "OMG!"

she whispered hard. "It's there."

Matt craned to look. Its claws were hooked around the delicate edges of the zoetrope, her nana's priceless heirloom. It twinkled as rays of afternoon sunlight pushed through the cage.

"Whoa!" Matt's heart did a backflip in his chest.

"No sudden moves," Miguel warned. "Starlings get aggressive, especially when you come close to their nests. I don't know if it's fledgling season."

"What's that?" Kylie asked.

"You know. Baby birds," Miguel answered proudly. "The mamas get very protective."

"How do you know so much about animals?" Kylie asked.

"I just do," he replied. "I just love them. Always have."

Matt surveyed the cage and the bird and its angry scowl. Its talons looked sharp—sharp enough to draw blood. He gulped. How many scratches would he get if he reached his hand in there right then, just grabbed the zoetrope and got it over with?

Kylic ducked and moved alongside the cage. "Will we need a key?" she whispered.

"No, it's just a lever," Miguel answered, waving her back to the group.

Danny zoomed in close, filming the kids and the bird. All roads led back to the camera. Matt wondered if birds attacked cameras but admitted that this would no doubt make a sweet climax in what was shaping up to be a pretty cool horror film. Frankie posed, dramatic, caught on camera, pretending to try to open the cage.

"Okay, so what's the plan?" Becca asked.

Miguel took charge, pulling everyone into a huddle.

"I can just open the cage and get it," Danny offered.

"It bites, remember?" Kylie said.

"And look at those claws." Matt's heart raced. He wasn't often that scared. He didn't like admitting to it, but terrible images flashed through his mind. Shorty the Starling scratching up his arms or biting his face.

Becca squared her shoulders. "I've got to rescue nana's zoetrope."

"Listen up!" Miguel took out his phone and opened an animal app. "I know a *lot* about starlings. . . . They like to fly in groups, so Shorty might be feeling lonely. Which means he could be cranky. He's got plenty of seed here. But he loves berries and some veggies as treats. Like Mr. Patrick's prized tomatoes. And he's always hungry. He's got that sharp beak and talons to make sure he can protect himself and eat what he wants."

"So are you saying we're going to get attacked?" Kylie asked, frustrated. "That one of us might get bitten?"

"Yes and no," Miguel responded.

"Will it destroy the zoetrope?" Becca asked, panic tucked into her voice.

"I hope not." Miguel put a supportive hand on her shoulder. "Now, here's what we're going to do. Starlings love fruit. Everyone pick one from the garden. We'll distract it long enough for Becca to grab the zoetrope." His big brown eyes found Becca's and she nodded in agreement.

Matt patted her shoulder. He remembered how stressed he'd felt when Ralphie was missing and the idea of Ralphie being in that cage with Shorty was almost too much. He knew Becca had to be freaking out inside.

Miguel led the way back to the garden. They weaved in and out of the different rows, scanning for fruits.

"Strawberries are in the front. The pears, bananas, oranges are in the greenhouse," Frankie informed the group, motioning to the glass greenhouse door, leading the others through the tight but colorful space.

Frankie suggested they grab a handful of strawberries from Ms. McKinney's patch and a couple of pears from the tree on the west side. Then they grabbed blueberries and raspberries from the vines on the trellis.

The kids placed all the goodies into a basket, closing the greenhouse door carefully and leading the way back to the aviary.

"Get small pieces we can slip through Shorty's cage bars first, okay?" Miguel said. "Lure him toward the door. Then I'll open the door and we make a trail. Hopefully, he'll drop the zoetrope, and then Becca can grab it. Then I'll get him back in his cage with one of our commands."

Everyone nodded and picked something. Becca grabbed a pear, golden brown, soft and tender. Matt grabbed strawberries and they made his mouth water and his stomach growl. It was already way past lunchtime. But they had to focus.

Frankie turned to approach Shorty's cage, but Miguel caught the back of their shirt. *"Wait!"*

They almost tumbled to the ground.

"Starlings are easily startled," Miguel explained. "We have to go one at a time. We can't crowd the cage. That's when they get soooooo upset."

Everyone nodded. They all tiptoed closer and closer to Shorty's cage, ducking to stay out of view.

"Danny, you first. You're closest," Miguel whispered, waving him forward.

Danny gulped and handed his camera to Kylie. "Get some footage of me, okay? Just push the red button."

"Really, Danny? Like, why right now?" Becca sounded exasperated.

"We might need it," he replied.

"That's true," Matt chimed in.

Becca rolled her eyes, but Kylie took the camera from him and looked through the lens. Danny was slow to step forward, clearly nervous. He raised his arm, flinching as he held out the cucumber. He waited a few moments, and Matt could see him counting in his head. But Shorty did not even look his way.

Danny scrambled back all sheepish and panicked. Becca handed him back his camera.

"A cucumber, really?" Miguel said. "That's *not* a fruit."

"Actually, it is," Frankie interjected, lifting their finger in the air with authority. "Technically, it grows from flowers and contains seeds, so it's botanically a fruit, but no one uses it like that."

"How do you know all this random stuff?" Becca asked.

"It's not *random*. It's food." A big smile consumed Frankie's freckly brown face, the first one Matt had really seen since this whole thing started.

"You're next, Frankie," Miguel said.

They lifted up a few cherry tomatoes. "These are fruits."

Matt watched as Frankie skulked along the edge of the aviary. Frankie was bolder in their approach, stepping forward with big careful strides, reaching their palm forward, wide open, a tiny cherry tomato sitting in the center, ripe for the picking. "These are supposedly Shorty's favorites," Frankie informed the others proudly.

Shorty squawked with delight and moved closer to the side of the cage to take the tomato. Becca and Matt almost squealed with delight, too, but Miguel flashed them a look to stay quiet. Frankie raced back to the group to silent cheers and high fives.

"Kylie, you're up." Miguel motioned for her to follow quickly in Frankie's footsteps.

She pulled her black hair back into a ponytail and handed Danny back his camera. Then she eased up to the cage with an orange that she'd peeled. Shorty watched her with his tiny beady eyes as her hand drew closer and closer to the bars.

Kylie bit into the orange, then tore at its flesh. She wiggled pieces near one cage bar. Shorty jumped for it, but she didn't let him have it. Instead, she teased him, moving it toward the door. The bird inched closer and closer, giving up its guard on the shiny zoetrope. Kylie dropped the piece inside as Shorty leaped for it, beak open, ready to bite down on the sweet flesh of the fruit. Or her finger.

Kylie scrambled back to the group, her breath ragged, her face flushed with excitement.

"Great job," Miguel said. "He's away from the zoetrope now."

"How do we get in the cage without being attacked?" Becca asked, palm warm, still clutching a handful of blueberries.

"Pure distraction." He opened his hand to show a small pile of blueberries and then nodded at his snake.

"You're going to let Nacho eat him?" Danny exclaimed in horror, hiding behind the camera again.

"No, no. Nacho doesn't even like birds . . . I don't think. Her favorites are mice." Miguel put his hands in the air.

"Becca, give your blueberries to Matt."

"But why?" she asked.

"You'll see."

Miguel pulled Matt forward. "We'll have Shorty try to get the blueberries and strawberries outside the cage so he's forced to leave the zoetrope behind. He's definitely got a sweet tooth." Miguel took a few of the blueberries and demonstrated on the ground, making a long trail from the base of the cage to the edge of the garden. "Once I open his cage, I'll lure him to leave." He gazed around as everyone nodded in agreement, then put on one of the long leather gloves hanging from the side of the cage.

Matt's heart pounded, his palms sweaty. This was it. The big moment. The zoetrope was right there, nearly within reach. They were so very close.

The crew worked to line up the berries in the perfect little trail.

Miguel crawled along the ground, staying out of Shorty's sight lines, and hovered just under the cage door. Frankie and Danny each squatted on the left side and the right side of the rectangular aviary. Kylie crept behind it. They all locked eyes, connected, ready to set their plan in motion. Matt stood near the trail, ready to add more berries if needed.

Becca took a deep breath. Miguel motioned for her to step forward and stand in front of the cage, right next to Shorty.

He squawked and scrambled back to the zoetrope.

"Now, Shorty, I need that back," she said nicely.

The bird gripped the metal edges of the zoetrope, which was now near the front of the cage.

"I don't know *who* put this in your cage, but it belongs to my nana," she said, her voice serious. "And you can't keep it."

Matt whispered under his breath, "C'mon, Becca. C'mon, Becca. I know you can do it."

Miguel reached his hand up and unhooked the cage gate. The door started to ease open. Becca fed Shorty a blueberry. He hopped a little closer. Then another one. He let go of the zoetrope.

Becca's eyes darted between Shorty and Nacho.

Everyone watched as the bird left the cage, its talons allowing him to climb along the bars and down to the ground. One by one it ate the berries. Matt worked quickly to add more.

"Now," Matt said to Becca. But too loud.

Shorty bolted upright, wings flapping hard and fast as Becca was about to reach inside to grab the zoetrope. It turned to attack Becca for going into its nest. With lightning speed, it darted to the zoetrope, grabbing it tight in his sharp talons.

"Oh no!" Becca shouted. "Don't fly off with it, don't fly off with it, don't fly off with it."

Shorty struggled to maintain flight. But the zoetrope glittered in his talons. Shorty circled with confusion. Then he

flew one way, then the other, just out of reach.

Miguel jumped in front of her with his glove and shouted, "Step down!"

The zoetrope dropped from his talons. It sailed through the air. Shorty darted straight to Miguel's glove.

Matt felt breathless as he watched the zoetrope plummet. Becca rushed forward, reaching her hands out to grab it.

She dived to catch it before it landed in the middle of the patch of grapevines in the garden. She hit the ground hard, out of sight, but then Becca bounced to her feet, clutching the zoetrope tight.

Matt breathed a huge sigh of relief, then let himself collapse for a moment, exhausted after all their adventures.

CHAPTER 19

Are You the GAME MASTER?

Becca

They all sat in the roof garden, exhausted, watching Shorty eat more fruit in his cage. Becca was thrilled to have her nana's zoetrope back. She clutched it to her chest and a sense of relief washed over her. The prize was in hand. Also, she was grateful Shorty hadn't flown away. She imagined him sailing off into the distance and how upset the whole school would be.

"Look what I found!" Kylie rushes over to Becca with a piece of paper.

Becca froze, afraid there was more to this game.

"It's another weird list." Kylie showed it to her. "It was in the cage."

WHO IS BECCA ZAMOLO?
"Gymnastics lets you forget sometimes that there is gravity!"
  1. *Her nana*
  2. *Graham crackers*
  3. *Clubhouses*
  4. *Puzzles*
  5. *Gymnastics*

"Don't you think it's weird that the Game Master made all these lists about us?" Matt asked.

"Yeah, but let's figure it out later. Let's get out of here," Danny said.

Frankie walked to the elevator and pushed the button. The elevator dinged and the door opened and they all climbed in.

Miguel hit the button for the first floor. "I don't know if I ever want to play a game again."

The elevator dinged open, and they walked toward the school entrance. *It had better be open*, Becca thought. They'd won the game. It was over. Time to go home.

That's when they heard it. The familiar crackle of the loudspeaker, which stopped them in their tracks.

"Well, well, my little friends." The Game Master's voice filled the lobby and their ears. "I didn't think you had it in you—but you worked as a team, solved all the challenges, and found Becca's beloved zoetrope. And so, per the rules of the game, I have to let you go." The voice cackled long and hard, eerie despite the sun and their win. "Until next time."

"Who are you?" Kylie shouted.

"Yeah! Show yourself." Frankie waved a fist in the air.

"I know it's you Vice Principal Pinter!" Matt screamed.

A single slip of paper floated down from the ceiling, seemingly from out of nowhere. And there it was, as Becca clasped it, still holding her zoetrope close: the GM logo.

The sounds of buckets and shelves falling filled the room. Everyone froze, then turned to gaze down the hall at the open maintenance office.

Matt took off running in that direction. Becca called after him but he wouldn't stop. They all followed.

"It's you!" Matt screamed.

Becca finally caught up and spotted Mr. Verdi. The school custodian. He held bundles of Game Master stickers.

"Why did you do this?" Becca's hand was on her hip and she felt like her mom after she'd discovered a mess and caught Becca in a lie.

Mr. Verdi's pale face turned bright red. He dropped the items in his hands. Sweat dripped down his cheeks like he'd just jumped out of the shower, and he was panting hard. He was covered in paint and that sticky red corn syrup and flour. He was wearing that familiar green uniform, the sun pouring in from the window, making his bald head gleam as he scratched it, confused and curious. "I . . . I . . ."

"Yeah, why?" Miguel stepped forward. Nacho perched on his shoulder, hissing.

"Why?" Matt muttered over and over under his breath.

Mr. Verdi put his hands up as if the kids were going to attack him.

"Danny, make sure to get this footage." Kylie stepped forward. "I want to make sure he can never lie about this."

"It's not my fault," he stammered out. "I mean . . . I didn't mean to."

"How do you not mean to?" Danny asked, the click of his camera echoing loudly.

Mr. Verdi started to pace in circles. He left a trail of flour. The explanation poured out of him. "This person said I had to do it. That if I didn't turn the school into an escape room that they'd . . . they'd . . ." His voice broke into two, and he started to sob.

Becca looked back and forth at each of her new friends. *What does this even mean? Why is he crying like this?* Her heart squeezed. Something was still wrong. Very wrong.

The school alarm blared. The sirens made everyone flinch and duck.

"We have to get out of here!" Mr. Verdi shouted.

They all darted out and into the hall.

Frankie, urgent, tried the lobby doors, pushing them wide open easily, as if they'd never been locked at all. The kids burst through the doors and into the sunshine, spilling out into a nearly empty parking lot. The afternoon sun pressed down on them and Becca felt nearly out of breath and frazzled. Her heart raced as her mind shuffled through a thousand questions.

Mr. Verdi started to run toward the cars.

"Stand in front of him!" Miguel shouted.

Everyone scattered left and right, making a circle around him. Now he couldn't leave without having to plow one of them over, and Becca stood firm. She wouldn't be moved. Not without a fight.

But looking at Mr. Verdi, all messy and sweaty and stressed out, Becca felt so far away from finding the answer. And there were few things she hated more than a puzzle she couldn't solve.

"Why did you do this?" Matt pressed. "You took her zoetrope and you stole my robot and you trapped us in school all day. That's got to be a dozen crimes."

"No, a hundred," Danny added.

"We should call the police!" Kylie threatened, holding up her phone. "We have a signal again."

"Tell us who the Game Master is," Becca asked. "Did you make these lists about us?"

Mr. Verdi sobbed. "I don't know. I . . . I . . . really don't. I just got all these emails and letters and then this kit arrived, and it had a map and instructions in it." He pulled out a crumpled paper and showed it to them.

"What are you all doing?" came a voice from behind.

They whipped around to find Principal Collins glaring at them. Her beautiful long braids hit her shoulders and her brown skin glistened in the sun. She was in her workout clothes and the frown on her face told them all she wasn't happy to have come to school from wherever she was before. "The alarm has gone off and there is unusual activity on the cameras."

Becca gulped as Principal Collins's hot gaze found her. "We . . . we . . . were trapped," she stammered out.

"I find that hard to believe." She scowled, pointing her finger in accusation. "There's a mess in *my* school and the cops are on the way because of the alarm. They will be looking for trespassers. I didn't think I'd find my own students. Just because you attend Hidden Vista doesn't mean you own the place."

Becca hated the disappointment in her voice. She loved Principal Collins and worked as an aide for her every spring when the student government activities started. She didn't wanted one of her favorite people in the whole building to hate her now. "It wasn't our fault."

"We were locked in," Frankie explained.

"And then there was this weird voice," Kylie added.

"It called itself the Game Master," Miguel said while Nacho slithered in close as Principal Collins glared.

"We had to do all these challenges," Danny said.

"But in the end, we worked together," Becca said, her voice firm, her grip on the zoetrope tight. "And won."

"This sounds like *some* story," the principal said, waving her hands in the air. "I should call all of your parents and tell them—"

Mr. Verdi burst into tears all over again and alongside the sobs came the truth. The story he'd told them earlier.

They all felt frozen in place.

Principal Collins's face held shock and alarm. As Mr. Verdi flailed in one big heap on the hot pavement, her eyes rested on each one of them. "I've got this, okay? Go on home. I'll take it from here."

"Yes, Principal Collins," they said in unison.

They watched as their principal tried to keep Mr. Verdi from thrashing around like a big toddler as he squealed and cried about what he'd done.

"My sister's here," Matt said, pointing to the school round-about driveway. "You all want a ride?"

"Wait!" Becca stood still. "Don't look, but there's someone staring at us out of a third-floor window," she said, her eyes wide, panicked. "Kylie, pretend to stretch and turn around. Then, Danny, act like you're adjusting your camera and turn it on. See if you can zoom in close. Matt, tie your shoe and try to look. Frankie, do the same. Miguel, pretend to be dealing with Nacho."

She heard each one of them gulp. "On the count of three. One . . . two . . . three . . ."

Becca pretended to yawn and lifted her head as Danny held up the camera, all casual, playing with lens. Then they froze for real. There was definitely a face in the window, spying down at them. Creepy.

Was that the *real* Game Master?

Who was it?

CHAPTER 20

Conspiracy Theories

Matt

"Let's get out of here!" Matt shouted after the figure left the window. He led the ragtag group across the school's grassy, quiet campus and to his sister's car. Ralphie sang a jumbled song as he jostled in Matt's arms. He sighed deeply, thrilled to have found him. But also still terrified that something was wrong with the robot. He had to get back to his workshop as soon as possible to make sure he was okay.

Miguel and Kylie were so relieved to see Matt's sister, they started to do an excited little jig, complete with spins and singsongs. Danny pulled out his camera, documenting their exit from school.

"I'm so over summer school," Frankie said.

"Where have you been?" Matt's sister, Sarah, leaned out of the window.

"It's a long story." He pushed his sweaty hair off his forehead. "Can we give them a ride? Everyone lives in the neighborhood."

"Sure," Sarah replied, unlocking the SUV and opening the trunk. "Backpacks and stuff in there to make room."

Becca untucked her zoetrope under her elbow and placed it carefully into the trunk. "Thanks," she whispered to Matt. "For, like, helping and everything."

He smiled sheepishly. "Thanks . . . for finding Ralphie." He found a spot on top of the mountain of backpacks and tried to tuck the robot in so he wouldn't get knocked around as his sister drove home.

The words felt like a truce between them. Like he finally understood a little bit more about her and she, a little more about him. Matt felt proud about that. He understood now what it felt like to almost lose something.

After the day's adventures, they all understood. He had been so worried about losing Ralphie, but today they stuck together through some pretty weird challenges. Like math problems and fake blood. And they'd won. He felt like for the first time he might have a group of friends. Maybe.

Matt's sister honked the horn. They all finished piling into the SUV, squeezing like clowns in a car. *Or people into a dumbwaiter*, Matt thought.

Sarah sailed out of the roundabout and paused at the stop sign. She gazed at the parking lot. "Why is Mr. Verdi rolling around on the pavement? It's so hot."

Everyone burst out laughing. "It's a long story," Matt replied.

Sarah shrugged her shoulders and put on the radio.

"I wonder who did all this," Kylie mumbled. "Makes me never want to go to school again."

Danny peered down at his camera. "Maybe if we go through the footage—"

Frankie lifted their palm, silencing him. "No more footage."

Becca sighed. "Does it matter anyway? We got out. We're all safe."

Danny examined his camera footage. "I can see a face, but it's not clear from this distance. Maybe I can clean it up later and get a better look once I edit it."

"Put it away for now," Frankie mumbled.

Matt turned around from the passenger seat, looking at his friends, who looked hot and exhausted. They looked like they'd been to war and back . . . or at least . . . if he was being honest, a really intense summer camp without air-conditioning.

Kylie leaned forward. "Who do you think did this?" she asked him.

Matt's mind flipped through suspects like Becca's zoetrope

flickering through its images. One after the other. "It could be anyone, really," he said quietly, watching his older sister yap on the phone as she drove, ignoring the carful of kids.

Kylie shrugged. "I just don't get why anyone would bother," she said. "It's just weird."

"I think it's Corey Ewing," Becca chimed in. "She's my nemesis from gymnastics camp! She saw me with the zoetrope when my mom visited during parents' weekend on April break. I know she had her eyes on it."

But how would Corey have managed it all?

"I think it's Mrs. Gupta," Danny replied, his eyes not veering from his camera as he played back the footage from the day. "She wanted to teach us a lesson, you know, for being loud and disruptive all summer. She's always loved games. Especially math ones." He wiped his brow, like his brain hurt. "All those games today were full of math."

"What about Mr. Castro? He's the one that's responsible for Shorty *and* the science lab," Miguel reminded them. "Totally him."

"Mr. Verdi could just be blaming someone else to throw off the focus from him," Kylie interjected, shaking her head. "He set it up. I mean . . . he told us that and everything."

Matt leaned back from the passenger seat. "But he was so upset. It didn't seem like he would be that sad if he actually *wanted* to torture us."

"But what about the person we saw? The one in the

window?" Frankie asked.

Maybe Kylie was right. Verdi did have every key. And every door was locked. Matt's stomach rumbled with a mix of hunger and fear. He wanted to forget about the whole thing, maybe even the whole summer. He had his robot back in one piece and Becca had her nana's zoetrope and they'd all gotten out safely—that's what mattered.

But something felt off. Like they were missing something.

CHAPTER 21

But Who Is the Game Master?

Becca

They all piled out of the car and into the quiet, sunny cul-de-sac of their neighborhood. Before splitting off and walking to their various houses, the six friends paused on the grassy roundabout. It was a relief to be home, to leave the games and the traps and the tension behind. Maybe they could enjoy the rest of their summer here in the peace of grassy lawns and gardens full of roses, tree houses and playhouses, and pool parties and barbecues.

Becca peered toward her driveway, worried for a moment, but Nana's car wasn't there yet. So there would be nothing to explain.

Becca was eager for home and lunch, for the quiet whir of

the AC. Maybe she'd spend the rest of the day curled up with a new book. But the others had gathered on Matt's lawn, a tight little circle. So she knew she had to stay.

"You okay?" Matt asked.

She nibbled her bottom lip. "Yeah, I guess."

Matt reached to put a hand on her shoulder, then pulled back, but then patted her. "Yeah, it's a lot," he said awkwardly.

They walked together to his lawn, where Matt's little brother had a lemonade stand set up. Mike even gave them all free lemonade. Slowly, they pieced together the day.

"Your mapmaking skills were totally on point, Kylie," Miguel said.

"And Danny's camera definitely helped," Kylie added.

"And I rocked it with the slime recipe," Frankie chimed in as they all laughed. "I mean, yeah, no slime. But Matt's clumsiness meant we found the clue."

Becca smiled. "And Miguel's animal training helped me get the zoetrope back," she said.

"I still don't get what the Game Master wanted with the zoetrope, though," Danny said, zooming in on it with the camera. "I mean, it's pretty. For a tin can."

"I'll show you one day," Becca said, rolling her eyes. "It's like an early version of a camera. It really is pretty cool."

Becca gripped the zoetrope tight to her chest, still afraid to let it get even an inch away from her grip.

"Okay, so let's take out all those Wanted posters and that

map we found," Matt directed, plucking the scroll from his back pocket.

He had Kylie help him unroll it.

It reminded Becca of a blueprint, a weird map of instructions for a building.

"It's the school," Kylie said, her eyes scanning the parchment, which looked very much like the paper map they'd found in the gym. It was drawn carefully with colored pencils and markers, the lines ruler straight, a scale for measurement.

"What is that?" Frankie asked, running their fingers over the different rooms.

Becca's eyes grew wide as she took in all the detailed plans: the clues, the traps, even her zoetrope—drawn right there in ink—sitting in the aviary in the roof garden. All carefully plotted and planned. And in the homeroom, six little figures smiling, unsuspecting, each bearing their names. Becca couldn't believe someone had set all this up. Could it really have been Mr. Verdi?

She'd barely ever even spoken to him at all. Except for that one afternoon when Nana was picking her up and she'd run past, rushing, nearly knocking him over. But it was such a small moment.

"I think it's Vice Principal Pinter," Matt proclaimed. "That man is mean and that's where we found the map."

"But I've never had a problem with him," Danny chimed in.

"Maybe Mr. Verdi is working for Mr. Kent," Matt proclaimed. "That man is mean."

"Mr. Kent the school secretary?" Becca asked.

"Yeah." Danny held his camera over the map and clicked Record, panning across it, capturing every detail.

"Yeah. He would have had access to the office." Matt pointed at the map; his dirty finger hovered over the area labeled "Vice Principal's Office." "It was like the Game Master's headquarters for sure. There were parchment and pens and supplies and these." He paused, dramatic, then pulled something small out of his pocket. The Game Master logo sticker. Like the ones they'd seen scattered throughout the school.

"'Headquarters,'" Kylie said aloud, pointing at the map.

"See!" Matt tapped the paper, too. Danny zoomed in.

"But why would he do it?" Miguel asked.

"How many times has he given you detention?" Matt asked.

"Like a hundred times. Even Nacho has gotten it, too. He hates snakes. Says they don't make good pets. He's rude." Miguel hugged his snake close to his chest.

Kylie swallowed hard. "He once confiscated all my mapping pencils. The kind used to draw this one." They all turned to peer at her.

"That's very convenient," Frankie said, their tone accusing.

"Mr. Verdi could be lying about someone forcing him to

do all of this," Becca added.

"What if Mr. Verdi was forced by one of *us*?" Frankie pressed.

"Come on," Matt said, nearly laughing. "You can't tell me you think it was Kylie."

Kylie frowned, but Frankie turned to Matt. "Actually, I thought it might be you," they declared. "And I'm not the only one."

Matt froze.

"It's so not Matt," Danny said just as Kylie interjected, "Why would Matt do this? Why would any of us?"

"You sure it's not *you*, Matt?" Frankie said. "You have the map. The stickers. And you do love a good prank. It's so obvious. But I might be able to forgive you if you fess up now."

Matt sighed, his face tomato sauce red. "I didn't do it. I hate being at school. Why would I ever want to trap myself there?"

"That's true," Becca replied. "He's always hated school." She didn't think he'd do anything like this. It would take too much work. He was the type of prankster that put fake spiders in your lunchbox or called your phone a thousand times breathing hard or sent you weird notes. Not going above and beyond like this. "Besides, what about the person we saw in the window?"

"I bet it's the head of maintenance. Mrs. Richards hates kids," Kylie said, her eyes scanning the map again. "The mission supply closet is even highlighted. See"—she tapped the page—"right here. It's got to be her. She has all the keys. Mr. Verdi works for *her*. She has to be the Game Master."

Frankie tapped their foot. "Why would she care enough to bother?"

"Frankie's right. I feel like the Game Master likes to have fun, though," Becca said. "Mrs. Richards is like what my nana calls a 'bah-humbug' kind of person. Hates everything."

Matt nodded in agreement with her. He couldn't imagine Mrs. Richards going to all this trouble to set up a game. No.

The Game Master was clever.

The Game Master was careful.

The Game Master was calculating.

Whoever it was, they'd plotted every move the kids made from beginning to end. They'd researched carefully, built challenges to fit their personalities, to work their fears. They knew the school, yes. But they knew the kids, too. Verdi didn't. Neither did Vice Principal Pinter. Not really. It was almost as if whoever set it up wanted to be their friend. The challenges all were things each one of them was good at or things they liked. There were those lists. Like this person was studying each of them.

The Game Master knew them, all of them, well.

A car entered the neighborhood. It was Becca's nana. Becca almost sighed with relief, holding the zoetrope even tighter again. "I should go," she told the others as they peered at the blueprint, still arguing.

Kylie smiled at her, reaching to touch the zoetrope again. "I'm just glad we got your nana's zoetrope back, Becca," Kylie said before turning to go home.

"It is really cool," Becca said as the others looked up. "Let me show you."

She adjusted the sides, then wound the little handle, watching the kids watch the images that flashed on the white picket fence. Matt whispered that it was cool and Becca smiled.

They were all riveted, especially Danny.

But then a phone rang, loud and shrill, distracting. It was Miguel's, and he answered, frowning as he listened. But they could all hear. It was Miguel's baby brother, Angel.

Becca gazed across the cul-de-sac at Miguel's house. The bright blue door swung open and out barreled a younger version of Miguel running across the yard and down the driveway in their direction. He was a head smaller, but with the same round face and buzzed hair and brown skin. And frantic as he raced across the street toward them.

"Migué! Migué!" he shouted. One small fist held up a piece of paper and the other clutched the handle of a pet carrier.

The screech in little Angel's voice sent a zip up Becca's spine.

"What is it, Angelito?" Miguel dropped to his knee.

"I . . . I . . ." His small chest heaved up and down as his breath came out in ragged breaths.

"Slow down," Becca said, putting a hand on his back. "It's okay."

They all huddled around the small boy.

"I . . . I found this letter." Angel handed Miguel a hand-written note. "And Elephant is gone."

"Who is Elephant?" Danny asked.

"My pet hamster." The small boy held up the empty carrier for Danny to inspect.

Miguel read the note aloud, his voice gathering worry.

You may have won the first round, my friends. But stay alert. Because the games have just begun.
—GM

"He's been hamster-napped," Danny said, pulling one of those familiar GM stickers from the little hamster crate.

Miguel looked stricken as little Angel sobbed into his shoulder. "You have to get him back. You have to," Angel said.

"Don't worry, Angel," Becca said. "We will."

Because Becca knew, as she looked at her ragtag crew of friends, that she could count on them to play as a team. And that meant, no matter what, they'd play to win.